ONE NIGHT
OF *Sin*

an After Hours novella

ONE NIGHT OF Sin

an After Hours novella

Elle Kennedy

Entangled Publishing, LLC
2614 South Timberline Road
Suite 105, PMB 159
Fort Collins, CO 80525
rights@entangledpublishing.com

Edited by Gwen Hayes
Cover design by Bree Archer
Cover photography by miljko/GettyImages

Manufactured in the United States of America

First Edition August 2014

ENTANGLED
BRAZEN

This one's for Viv.

Chapter One

She was staring at him again.

Gage felt those big blue eyes burning a hole in his back, and when he turned around, there she was. Still seated in the velvet booth across the room, half listening to her male companion while her curious gaze remained focused on another man. On *him*.

It had been two years since the club's grand opening, which meant two years' worth of shifts, but Gage could honestly say this was the first time he'd gotten hard on the job. Although beautiful women poured into Sin on a nightly basis, not one had ever triggered such a visceral response in him.

Forget about it. Too young, too sweet, and too out of your league.

Yup, the cynical voice in his head was right on the money. Little black dress and fuck-me red heels aside, the brunette in the booth exuded a good-girl vibe that almost made him feel guilty for checking her out. A man like him would corrupt her in a heartbeat. Taint her. Lead her down a path of damnation to a wicked place where girls like her didn't belong.

And bad idea, thinking about all the wicked things they could do together, not when he was already semi-erect. Now there was nothing *semi* about it—his cock was at full salute and pushing against his fly.

Gritting his teeth, he turned away and swept his gaze over the VIP lounge. It was crowded tonight, more than usual for a Thursday, but things had been tame so far. Granted, it was only midnight. In his experience, Asshole Hour didn't start until closer to 1:00 a.m., after too much booze or drugs or sexual tension tipped a customer's conduct scale from *harmlessly wild* to *dangerously stupid*. As head of security, Gage was tasked with making sure that didn't happen—or stepping in if it did.

He edged toward the railing and studied the cavernous main room ten feet below. The dance floor was packed, every table and booth occupied, and the intermittent strobe lighting illuminated a sea of flushed, euphoric faces. Gage spotted several couples making out in the shadows, and those who weren't into PDA were probably getting into all sorts of trouble in the curtained alcoves situated throughout the club. Sin always drew a wild crowd—folks of all ages flocked to the club for a night of boozing, dancing, and even screwing if they didn't make a spectacle out of it.

Everything on the floor looked fine, and Gage knew his bouncers would notify him over the comm if that changed. For now, no problems seemed to be brewing in the air.

"BMOC over there just asked if we offer party favors." Carla sidled up to Gage, her red-painted lips close to his ear as she gave him the heads-up.

His eyes narrowed at the pretty waitress. "What kind of party favors? And which big man on campus are we talking about?"

"I'm pretty sure he's looking for pussy. The expensive kind." The blonde gave a discreet tilt of the head. Right in the direction of the back booth.

Gage turned, expecting his gaze to collide with a pair of hungry blue eyes, but the brunette was gone. Only her date remained, tapping his fingers on the tabletop, a smug look pasted on his chiseled face. The kid couldn't have been older than twenty-two or twenty-three, but he exuded an air of entitlement that was impossible to miss. He was a Very Important Person, at least in his own eyes.

"Who is he?" Gage asked.

"Kat said he's some big shot's kid. That's how he got up here."

The younger guy's dark eyes were checking out every woman in the lounge. He made no attempt to hide it, either, as if it was his *right* to leer.

Gage felt vindicated by the knowledge that the kid's beautiful date had ditched him.

"Tell him we don't sell skin here," he said coolly. "If he can't find a girl who'll fuck him for free, he can go out on the street corner like any other john."

Carla snorted. "Gotcha."

Man, he really hated some of the clientele that frequented Sin. Every night he encountered at least one rich, pretentious ass who thought the world owed him something. Case in point—this smug-faced creep inquiring about procuring the services of a whore.

As part owner, Gage supposed he had the right to throw the guy out, but Reed and AJ would tear him a new one if they found out he was sending away big spenders.

And big spender, indeed. Gage glanced back in time to see Carla delivering a six-hundred-dollar bottle of whiskey to the table. And the douche bag was now making eyes at the cute, not-a-prostitute redhead seated at the VIP bar. Good. She ought to occupy him for a while.

Gage touched his earpiece. "Yo, Jesse, get up here and

take over. Gonna pop out for a cigarette."

The bouncer's baritone voice crackled in his ear. "Got it, boss."

He waited until he spotted Jesse's close-cropped head weaving through the crowd. In between flashes of strobe, Gage saw the crowd part without delay for the muscular man, which made him smile. He'd handpicked all the bouncers himself, with only two required traits in the hiring process: reliable and intimidating as fuck. Jesse fit both of those to a T.

As the other bouncer ascended the steps up to the lounge, Gage headed for the emergency exit on the other side of the room. He strode down the narrow staircase, emerging a moment later in the alley behind the building.

He rummaged in his pocket for his e-cigarette, lifted his head—and froze.

His blue-eyed angel sat eight feet away. Slender body up on the wooden crate next to the staff door, chestnut-brown hair falling over one shoulder, dress riding up her thighs to reveal long, silky legs.

He sucked in a breath. Lord, she was even more appealing up close. Not beautiful in the Hollywood sense, but intriguingly attractive in a very *real* way. The enormous blue eyes were her best feature, and her mouth was just pouty enough to conjure up the image of plump lips wrapped around his dick.

Gage cleared his throat. "You shouldn't be out here."

She jumped at the sound of his voice, head swiveling and gaze flying to his. She instantly hopped off the crate, smoothing out the front of her dress as a frown creased her lips. "Why not?"

"A pretty girl all alone in an alley at midnight—I don't think it needs much more explanation than that." He inhaled a quick drag of the e-cigarette. The mint-flavored vapor was no substitute for a real smoke, and he wasn't sure why he even bothered with it.

"I just needed some air." Her voice was huskier than he'd imagined it would be. Sexier. "I'll go back inside soon."

Wait—she'd only come outside for air? And her date had been asking about *prostitutes* in her absence? Wow. Real stand-up guy.

"It's so crowded in there," she added.

"Nightclubs usually are," he said dryly.

"Yeah, I guess they are. I'm not much of a clubber, but Mick wouldn't take no for an answer. He said I haven't lived until I've gone to Sin." A sigh slipped out. "It's our first date…"

Gage waited for her to continue. When she didn't, he filled in the rest. "And you're not at all into him."

"Why do you say that?"

His gaze slid back to hers, slow and purposeful. "Because if you were, you wouldn't have been eye-fucking me all night."

Her breath hitched, cheeks growing the most appealing shade of pink.

He had to laugh. "Am I wrong?"

The denial he'd expected didn't come. "No, you're not wrong."

Christ. There were so many things he could say to that, so many things he could do. Dirty, dirty words and dirty, dirty acts. But he reined in every single wicked urge. Just because her mere proximity had turned his lower body into a raging inferno didn't mean he would give in to the burn. He was a grown man. More than capable of controlling his base impulses.

"I'm Skyler," she said, after his silence had dragged on for far too long.

He nodded.

"Maybe you're new to civilized society, but normally when people introduce themselves, you reply by providing your own name." She arched one perfectly defined eyebrow.

"Is that right?" His lips twitched. "Well, what makes you

think I'm at all civilized, Skyler?"

That made her falter. She bit her lower lip. Tucked a strand of hair behind her ear, and the scent of her shampoo floated his way. She smelled like green apples. A sweet and feminine fragrance, serving as a reminder that he shouldn't be out here talking to her.

"How old are you, sweetheart?" His voice came out rough.

"Well, my ID held up at the door, so I'm over twenty-one if that's what you're worried about. Twenty-four, actually. In some cultures that would make me a spinster."

Gage swallowed a laugh. There was something truly refreshing about her sarcasm, especially when contrasted with the flush of her cheeks and the way she fidgeted with her hands. She didn't belong here. Not at this club, not even in this neighborhood. She should be nestled between crisp white sheets right about now, snuggled next to a wholesome man while the two of them watched late-night talk shows before bed.

"Go back inside," he said gruffly. "Your date's probably wondering where you are."

That made her snicker. "I doubt it. I think he wrote me off the second he realized I wasn't going to fuck him tonight."

Gage's cock jerked in his pants. Jesus. That angel mouth wasn't allowed to say things like that. Not in front of *him*, a man whose inner devil could be summoned at the drop of a hat.

"Go back inside," he repeated.

"Why? You don't like talking to me?" Hands planted on her slim hips, she moved closer, a pensive look on her face.

He shrugged. "I don't like talking, period."

"Huh. So what *do* you like to do?"

Gage met her eyes in another long, deliberate stare. Leaving no question as to what he enjoyed doing.

She visibly swallowed. And then she startled the hell out of him.

"So maybe that's what we should do."

A laugh rumbled out of his chest. "You're playing with fire, baby."

"Am I?"

She had the nerve to lick her lips. He didn't think she'd done it as an intentional taunt, but damn, the response to seeing her tongue dart out was instantaneous. His erection pulsed against his zipper, hard and persistent, like it was trying to tunnel its way out of his pants and into her pussy.

Gage took a breath, trying to ease the ache down south. Nope, he wasn't giving in, wasn't going to acknowledge the awareness prickling over his flesh. He was fighting in two days, and he didn't like to screw before a match. The frustration fueled him, gave him the edge he needed to send an opponent to his knees.

But at the moment, *he* wanted to be the one on his knees. With his head underneath Skyler's skimpy dress, his face buried between her legs as he licked her up until she screamed.

"Yes," he rasped. "You're definitely playing with fire."

"Maybe I like fire, did you ever think of that? Maybe I *want* to get burned."

God help him. The defiance in her voice was almost as big of a turn-on as the heat in her eyes. She was looking at him like she wanted to eat him up. Like he was already naked and pumping inside her.

"You don't even know me," he muttered.

Her voice never wavered. "I don't care."

Gage stared at her again. He couldn't figure her out. She was young, just as he'd suspected. Sweet, too. But there was no mistaking the passion heating her gaze.

He took a step toward her. "You don't care that you don't know my name."

"No." One word, low and breathy.

He moved in closer, slowly backing her up into the brick wall. She let him. Her heels clicked softly on the pavement as she walked backward, until her body connected with the hard surface and she had nowhere else to go.

"You don't care that you've only known me for five minutes."

"No."

Gage kept a solid five inches between them, but at the rate his dick was thickening, it would find a way to breach the distance sooner rather than later.

He brought his lips close to her ear and enjoyed the way she shivered. "Why not, Skyler? Why don't you care?"

"Because…" She had to tip her head back to meet his gaze. "Because I like how this feels."

"How what feels?"

"*This*. Being bad. I've never done anything like this before."

No, he doubted she had. Yet nothing in her expression told him she didn't want it. Her face held a combination of heat, lust, and fascination. Her breathing came out labored, breasts practically spilling out of her dress with the rise and fall of her chest, and he certainly didn't miss the blush on her creamy skin or the insistent throb of her pulse at the base of her throat.

"You're turned on," he said softly.

"Yes." She squeezed her lips together, and from the way her whole body clenched, he suspected she'd squeezed her thighs together, too.

Fucking hell. He wanted to pry her legs open and slip his fingers inside her, discover just how turned on she really was.

As if she'd read his mind, her body relaxed, and his gaze dropped in time to see her stance widen, those red stilettos gleaming in the moonlight slicing into the alley. God. She'd spread her legs, blatantly giving him permission to take what he wanted.

"Why aren't you scared of me?" he murmured.

"Should I be?"

"Maybe." Unable to help himself, he touched her face, rubbing her bottom lip with his thumb.

She gasped quietly, then leaned into his touch.

Son of a bitch. This woman was liable to kill him. He'd never met anyone who was so ready to be *fucked*. Her arousal surrounded him like an enticing haze, quickening his pulse and fogging his mind.

"Don't act like you don't want it." Big blue eyes, gleaming with challenge, peered up at him. "Earlier when I was looking at you...you were looking right back. You liked what you saw."

Without breaking eye contact, he erased those five inches of distance by thrusting his thigh between her legs. He knew the second she felt his erection pressing into her, because she gave another sharp intake of breath.

"Tell me your name," she whispered.

Gage rotated his hips and fought a groan as a rush of heat flowed through him. What the hell was happening to him? He couldn't remember the last time he'd wanted someone this bad.

"Why should I?" His lips traveled to her ear, tongue slipping out to lick the delicate lobe. He chuckled when her hands shot up to cling to his shoulders. She tried pulling him closer, but he didn't let her. "I don't think you want to know my name," he mocked. "I think it would ruin the fantasy."

Skyler wrinkled her forehead. "What's the fantasy?"

He rubbed his aching cock over her pelvis, loving the way her eyes widened with pleasure. He grasped one long leg and propped it on his hip, deepening the contact, ignoring the voice in the back of his head. The one shouting for him to stop. Dry-humping a stranger outside his place of business was a stupid idea, but this woman had unleashed his carnal caveman.

"What's the fantasy?" she repeated, a twinge of anxiety in her voice.

He shoved a hand in her hair, yanking hard on one thick strand before lazily twining it around his fingers. "Getting fucked by a stranger. That's what you want, isn't it? For me to fuck you right here, right now, against this wall. Isn't that what you want, Skyler?"

The anguished noise she made was the sexiest thing he'd ever heard. "Y-yes. That's what I want."

A dark laugh slid out. He licked a path from her ear down to her neck, latching his mouth on her hot flesh. Lord, she was burning up. And she'd started grinding her lower body against him, rocking hard, each desperate glide over his cock sending him closer to the edge. Hell, at this rate, he'd come in his pants before he even took his dick out.

But no. No. He may have boarded this bad idea train, but now it was time to derail it.

Except he couldn't stop, couldn't think straight, couldn't concentrate on anything but the warm, willing woman in his arms. He trailed kisses up her throat, paused briefly to nibble on her jaw, then zeroed in on that pouty mouth. Screw it. One kiss. Just to find out if she tasted as sweet as he suspected.

But holy hell, it was even better than he could've ever imagined. The moment their mouths met, every shred of common sense flew out the window. Her lips were warm and pliant and eager as hell as she kissed him back like a woman starved. Her body melted against him like hot butter, slender arms wrapping around his neck as her tongue greedily slid into his mouth. Gage slicked his tongue over hers, groaning when a shock wave of lust roared through him.

He tugged on her hair, angling her head so he could drive

the kiss deeper. He was a fucking goner. Maybe he could've stopped it—if she didn't taste so good, if her body wasn't so soft and warm, if her throaty moans weren't vibrating against his lips. But stopping was impossible now, not when she kept swirling her hungry little tongue over his and riding his thigh with zero abandon.

His mouth stayed locked with hers, even as he lowered his hand to his zipper. Goddamn it, he *had* to be inside her. Right fucking now—

"Uh, boss?"

The male voice sliced into his ear like an electric current and promptly jump-started his brain.

He tore his lips away from Skyler's. Breathing hard, trying to recover from that mind-blowing kiss.

"Shit," he mumbled, then sucked in another breath and touched his ear. "What is it, Jerry?"

Skyler blinked. "Huh?"

He gestured to his earpiece, then focused on the amused voice of the man who monitored the club's security booth. "Reed wants to know if we should shut off camera two. You know, for privacy."

Aw hell.

Gage stifled a curse, his gaze moving to the camera mounted right above the staff entrance. The blinking red light was practically waving at him, a reminder that even though they were alone in the alley, they weren't *actually* alone.

"We don't mind watching, though," another voice piped up, this one belonging to Reed Miller, Gage's best friend and one of Sin's co-owners.

Rather than answer, Gage shifted around and gave his audience the finger.

Then he shut off the feed and turned to Skyler, whose face still held the flush of arousal. "Go inside and find your date. Get him to drive you home."

"No."

The fortitude in her eyes was dangerous. And she still hadn't fixed her dress. It was bunched around her waist, revealing firm thighs and pale skin and a perfect view of her panties. They were red, just like the shoes, and so skimpy his mouth went dry, because he knew it would take no effort at all to rip them off her. With his teeth.

He fought to speak past the lust clogging his throat. "The fantasy isn't gonna play out, Skyler. I'm not the right man for the job."

She stepped close and pressed her palm over his groin, cupping his erection with a boldness that surprised him. "I don't know…I think you might be *exactly* the right man."

He thrust into her hand. Just once, just one second of contact, before he eased out of her grip and tipped his head at the camera. "Do you really want to put on a show for my partners? Because that's what we're doing."

"Partners?"

"I'm co-owner of this joint. And even though my behavior these last ten minutes might say otherwise, I don't make it a habit of screwing around on the job." He paused meaningfully. "And you don't strike me as the kind of girl who screws around at all."

She had the nerve to smirk at him. "I'm not a virgin, if that's what you're implying."

"I'm not implying anything." He smothered his growing aggravation. Christ, the one time he tried acting like a gentleman, and look where it got him. "I don't know you, but I'm pretty sure you don't go around doing strangers in public. I have no clue why you decided to do it tonight—maybe it's that asshole Mick, maybe you had too much to drink. But the best thing for you to do right now is go home, Skyler."

"Why do men always assume they know what's best for a woman?" she demanded. "And FYI? I didn't drink anything but water tonight, and I was over Mick about five minutes after he picked me up. You want to know why I'm out here with you? Because I was attracted to you and decided to act on it. For once in my life I was acting on impulse, not thinking about consequences or overanalyzing things." Her gaze sharpened as she studied him. "You, on the other hand, you're all about impulse, aren't you? You strike me as a man of action." There was a beat. "I'm kind of surprised you wimped out at the thought of getting busy in front of a camera."

He clenched his teeth. "I didn't wimp out."

"Really? Are we having sex right now?" Another beat. "Nope, I didn't think so."

She finally straightened her dress, much to his overwhelming relief. Those red panties had come dangerously close to stealing his common sense again.

Gage sighed. "You really should go."

"Oh, I will. The moment's over, anyway." Her blue eyes flickered with something that made him uneasy. "What would you do if I came back tomorrow night?"

A groan lodged in his throat. He was trying to do the honorable thing, to save her from the regrets she'd undoubtedly have after sleeping with a total stranger, but the infuriating woman didn't seem at all appreciative of his caution.

"You shouldn't do that," he said in a low voice.

"Why not?"

"Because you're right. I'm impulsive, and I don't usually show much restraint. No matter what you think, stopping this, stopping what we were about to do, was damn hard for me."

She glanced at the bulge in his pants. "I can see that."

Gage grasped her chin, forcing her gaze away from his aching cock and up at his face. "Don't tempt me, all right? You're beautiful, Skyler. Beautiful and sexy and so goddamn tempting. If you come back, I won't be able to control myself next time."

"Is that a promise?"

Oh *hell*. He released her, taking a hasty step backward. "Go," he muttered. "I mean it."

He waited for an argument, but miraculously, she didn't give him one. Instead, she smirked again before sauntering away, hips swaying with each step she took.

His gaze followed her all the way to the door, staying glued to her slender form as she walked back into the club. And then the door swung shut and she was gone.

But Gage had the unnerving feeling that he hadn't seen the last of her.

Chapter Two

"I did something crazy last night," Skyler announced.

Lacey snickered. "Yeah, you went out with Mick the Dick. We know."

"No, not that. I did something even crazier." She dragged her tired body to the kitchen counter, poured herself a cup of coffee, and took a much-needed sip.

She hadn't slept a wink after Mick had dropped her off last night. Instead, she'd spent a solid hour on the computer, followed by several more lying in bed and thinking about the gorgeous sex god who'd made her feel honest-to-God *lust* for the first time in her life.

Gage Holt.

Yep, she'd Googled him. It hadn't been too difficult to find him after he'd let it slip that he owned the club. Two minutes was all it took to pull up a newspaper feature about the grand opening of Sin, with a picture of Gage and his two partners underneath the headline. Another search, and she'd discovered that he was a former fighter. He'd fought on the professional mixed martial arts circuit since the age of eighteen, winning a ton of matches before retiring a few years back. She hadn't found any online footage of his fights, so she'd had to satisfy herself by staring at his picture from the newspaper article.

And seeing his face, even in grainy black and white, had only reignited the fire of lust he'd set inside her.

"Sky?"

May's voice snapped her from her thoughts. She gulped down some more coffee, the caffeine successfully turning her brain from muddled to alert.

"Sorry, what?" She turned to face her roommates.

"I asked what could possibly be crazier than going out with Mick," May said dryly.

Skyler drifted to one of the stools around the cedar work island and flopped down next to Lacey. She was kind of surprised that all three of them were even in the same room. She'd shared the old Victorian house with Lacey and May for four years, but their hectic schedules didn't usually align to allow them to spend much time together. Still, no matter how busy they all were, the two women were Skyler's closest friends.

And they always gave her damn good advice.

"I made out with a total stranger at the club," she confessed.

Two jaws hit the kitchen floor.

"You're shitting me." Lacey started to laugh. "You had an anonymous hookup? That's *so* not your style."

"I know." She wrapped her fingers around her mug. "It just sort of…happened. Somehow."

"Uh-huh. You just opened your mouth and *somehow* a dude's tongue slipped inside it," May teased.

She offered a sheepish grin. "Fine, there was more to it than that. I went outside for some air—Mick was acting like a total ass, by the way. I was dying to get away from him."

"I told you not to go out with him," Lacey grumbled. "Didn't you learn anything from my experience in freshman year? The asshole *forgot* he asked me out on the same night he asked someone else, and when the other chick and I showed up at the restaurant at the same time, he tried to convince us to have a threesome!"

"Seriously, why did you even agree to go on a date with that jerk?" May sighed.

Because he asked.

Skyler bit back the words, not wanting to admit just how dismal her love life had become. School and work kept her so busy she didn't have time to meet many men, and all the ones who *did* hit on her? No thank you. The guys in her psychology classes just tried to "analyze" her, and the male customers who flirted with her at the restaurant were usually creeps.

Sad as it was, Mick the Dick was the first viable candidate she'd come across in months. When they'd bumped into each other at the university library and he'd asked her out, the thought of actually leaving the house had eclipsed her memories of Mick's douche bag college days. She'd wanted so badly to crawl out of the work-and-school rut and have some fun.

No, it was more than that, she realized. She'd wanted a *change*. She'd wanted new and exciting instead of old and boring. Mick might have been a jerk in college, but he'd also been impulsive and larger than life. A part of her had hoped that maybe those traits would rub off on her.

And boy, had they. She'd all but thrown herself at a complete stranger—it didn't get more impulsive than that.

"I was hoping Mick might have grown up since then," she answered. "But you were right. He's still the same cocky, self-absorbed jerk."

"And your mystery man?" May prompted, her blue eyes twinkling. "Was he, um, *cocky*?"

Skyler's thighs clenched as the memory of last night floated through her head. God. She'd almost melted into a puddle of mindless need when Gage had started grinding his rock-hard erection into her.

"He was…intense," she admitted. "One minute we were talking in the alley—I don't even remember what about—and the next we were up against the wall pawing at each other."

Her roommates exchanged wide grins. "About time," Lacey declared. "I keep telling you, celibacy isn't healthy."

"I'm not celibate. It's just been a while since I met anyone I wanted to sleep with."

May frowned. "Why didn't you sleep with Mystery Man?"

Annoyance rose in her throat. "Because he said no! He stopped it before things got too hot."

After a long pause, both women were laughing again.

"So he was perfectly cool with playing tonsil hockey in an alley but then refused to take it further?" May said.

"Pretty much."

May looked even more bewildered. "But you, *you*, Skyler Thompson, wanted it to go further?"

Her friends were right. Casual hookups weren't her style—hell, she didn't even put out on the first date—and yet she couldn't muster up a single regret about last night.

Gage Holt… Oh boy, everything about him turned her on. His smoldering gray eyes. That ruggedly handsome face. The dark stubble dotting his strong jaw. And his body…holy moly. He'd towered over her, every inch of him deliciously hard and rippled. Broad shoulders, muscular chest, long legs.

But she'd been attracted to more than his looks. It was also his…*presence*. When he'd trapped her against the wall with his massive body, the most incredible thrill had shot through her. She'd never been dominated like that before, and it embarrassed her to admit just how badly she'd liked it.

"I know, it's totally unlike me," she confessed.

Lacey snickered. "Big time."

"But it was so…*exciting*." She sighed. "These past couple months I started noticing how boring my life has become, and I just wanted to try something different, step out of my comfort zone, you know? And then my stranger came along and he was so…God, he was…" She couldn't even come up with any more adjectives to describe how incredible the man was. "Honestly, in that moment? I would have gotten naked in a heartbeat. I would have done anything that man wanted." The confession heated her cheeks, and she had to avert her eyes.

"Aw, she's blushing," Lacey teased. "It was *that* hot, huh?"

"Yes." Skyler released a glum breath. "I think he was trying to do the 'right thing'"—she used air quotes—"by stopping. He pretty much said I was a 'good girl'"—air quotes again—"and that I'd end up regretting it if I did anything with him, which is pure and total *bullshit*."

She punctuated the last word with more quotes, which made Lacey roll her eyes. "You have no idea how to use air quotes, babe."

"And was he really that far off the mark?" May chimed in. "Face it, Sky. You *are* a good girl. And that's not a bad thing. I mean, you're nice, funny as hell, crazy-protective of the people you care about. You're frickin' awesome. But you're not the one-night-stand type. He probably saved you a whole bunch of postcoital regrets by not doing you."

"Just because I haven't had a one-night stand before doesn't mean I'm not the type for it. What if I try it and end up loving it? What if I discover I really like the whole wham-bam-thank-you-dude aspect of it?" Skyler suddenly stuck out her chin. "You know what? You guys have convinced me. I'm going back there tonight."

May groaned. "That wasn't what I was advising *at all*. I think it's a *good* thing you didn't sleep with the guy."

"Actually…" Lacey grinned. "I'm with Sky on this. She never does anything fun. It's always work and school, school and work. Be a little wild, babe. I fully support your decision to go out and bang your stranger."

A laugh popped out. "Thank you. And you"—she turned to May—"I give you permission to say *I told you so* if it all blows up in my face."

"Deal." May scraped her chair back. "Okay, gals, it's been fun, but I've gotta get ready for work."

"Me too." Lacey hopped off the stool, chugging the rest of her coffee on her way to the sink. "I'm doing a forty-eight-hour shift at the hospital, so you won't see me for a couple days."

Skyler glanced over in concern. "Try to squeeze in some sleep, will you? Last time you worked a shift that long, you were a zombie for weeks afterward."

"Yes, Mom."

A moment later, Skyler found herself alone in the kitchen. She didn't mind it, though. Her arrangement with May and Lacey suited her just fine. They each did their own thing—Lacey had her residency at Boston General, May was finishing her art history master's and did restorations at the museum, and Skyler was halfway through with her master's in psychology. But despite their chaotic schedules, the friendship they'd formed during freshman year of college had remained strong.

As she went to grab another cup of coffee, her mind drifted back to Gage. The entire encounter had been exhilarating and terrifying, and she wanted to see him again, damn it. To hear his gruff voice tickling her ear, feel those big hands on her body.

Was she crazy to chase after a man she didn't know? A man who hadn't even told her his name?

Yeah, probably. But she didn't care. She'd *thought* she'd

known what arousal felt like. She'd *thought* she'd known what it was like to be attracted to someone.

And last night revealed that she'd had no frickin' clue.

Every spark of desire she'd ever experienced in her life—they were nothing compared to the wicked sensations Gage Holt had evoked in her.

If you come back, I won't be able to control myself next time.

His deep voice rasped in her head, making a shiver dance up her spine. She really hoped he'd meant every word.

Because she was definitely holding him to that.

• • •

"Where's AJ?" Gage glanced around Reed's office, confused by AJ Walsh's absence. Their third partner never missed a Friday night briefing.

"He took the night off," Reed answered. "He's got plans with the girlfriend."

Gage rolled his eyes. "You can say her name, man. She's not Voldemort, you know."

"Christ. Your boy-wizard references freak me out, bro. Cage fighters aren't allowed to read Harry Potter."

"I'm a bouncer, not a cage fighter." He couldn't mask his frustration, but rerouted the subject before his friend dived into another lecture about how *he* was the one who'd willingly put himself in his current predicament. "Anyway, her name is Darcy, and one of these days you're gonna have to suck it up and be nice to her."

Reed looked hurt. "I *am* nice to her." His dark blue eyes flickered with worry. "Why, did she say I wasn't?"

"No, but I'm sure she's noticed you never string together more than a sentence or two when she's around."

Reed's body language revealed discomfort, and Gage

glimpsed something in his friend's eyes that he couldn't quite decipher. Before he could say anything more, Reed promptly shifted gears.

"Let's get the business shit out of the way—do you have a lead on who's pushing E in the club?"

"Nope. You?"

Reed rounded the desk and flopped down in his leather chair, raking both hands through his messy black hair. "No clue. Are the guys keeping their eyes open?"

Gage nodded. "Nobody's seen a thing."

"And yet we've talked to dozens of people who claim they bought the stuff right here in the club." Reed ground out an expletive. "We need to find this asshole."

Gage shared his partner's anger. With the number of people who packed the club on a nightly basis, it was impossible to stop customers from coming in with a few lines of coke or some tablets of E, not unless they thoroughly searched everyone at the door. Which meant they had no choice but to tolerate some drugs floating around Sin. But someone selling the stuff directly from the club was a big fat no-no. The cops would shut them down in a heartbeat, and Gage wasn't about to lose the hefty profits the club brought in.

"I'll tell the guys to be extra alert tonight," he said, sinking into the armchair across from the desk. "Once we figure out who the dealer is, it'll be easy to put him out of commission."

"Good." Reed grabbed a pack of Camels from the desk and lit a cigarette, then proceeded to blow a cloud of smoke in Gage's direction.

He winced, trying not to inhale. "You just have to flaunt it in my face, don't you? I'm trying to quit, asshole."

"You've been trying to quit for two years."

"This time it'll stick."

"Ha. *Sure.*" His friend suddenly broke out in a grin. "Hey, so when can I expect the deets about your lady friend? You know, the one you almost boned in the alley yesterday?"

He stifled a sigh. It had been too much to hope that Reed wouldn't bring it up. "It was nothing," he mumbled.

Reed smirked. "Didn't look like nothing."

"Well, it was."

Liar.

All right, so maybe it had been the furthest thing from *nothing*. Maybe he'd stayed awake half the night thinking about Skyler. Maybe he'd jerked off three times before the arousal had finally dissipated, and even then, it still lingered under the surface, waiting for any opportunity to rear up again.

But he didn't regret sending her away. If she didn't have the word "relationship" written on her forehead in huge block letters, he might've given in and taken her to bed, but he got the feeling she was the kind of girl who wouldn't be satisfied with anything less than a commitment. Well, Gage didn't do commitments. He wasn't cut out for relationships — past experience had proved that — and he wasn't about to risk breaking another heart.

Women like Skyler deserved better than a breathless, hurried screw outside a nightclub, and besides, she was only twenty-four, which made her way too young for him. Not that he was an old man at the ripe age of thirty, but Lord, he felt that way sometimes. Felt like he'd lived ten lifetimes already.

"Fine, I'll drop it," Reed said. "Just know that I wholeheartedly approve of last night or any future nights you might spend with your mystery girl. It was kinda hard to tell from a security feed, but she looked hot."

Gage rolled his eyes again. Of course Reed approved. *Hot* was the only requirement the guy had for hooking up, with *temporary* coming in at a close second. Reed was a player to the core, and had been from the moment Gage met him, back when they were two punk-ass teenagers growing up in South

Boston. They'd both dreamed of becoming professional MMA fighters, though Gage's style leaned toward boxing while Reed was an out-and-out brawler, not above fighting dirty. And they'd both retired at the same time, taking the cash they'd earned over the years to open the club.

"Are you fighting tomorrow?"

The abrupt demand summoned an inward groan. "Yeah." He kept his tone vague.

"Only one more after that, right?" Reed asked carefully.

"Two more."

"And then you and Mitch are square?"

"Yep."

"You sure about that?"

He met Reed's uneasy expression head-on. "Damn sure."

After a beat of silence, his friend heaved out a breath. "I sincerely hope Denny appreciates what you do for him, bro."

"He does."

"Yeah? 'Cause I don't see a lot of gratitude coming your way." Reed took a quick drag, this time polite enough to exhale in the opposite direction. "Look, you and I go way back. Which means Denny and I go way back too. And in all these years, not once have I heard a *thank you* leave that little bastard's mouth."

Gage stiffened. "Watch it, man. He's my brother."

"Doesn't make him any less of a bastard." Reed leaned forward and snuffed out his cigarette in the ashtray. "The way I see it, a real man cleans up his own messes."

He didn't answer. *Couldn't* answer. Because Reed was right. Denny always took the easy way out, and for Denny, the easy way meant handing his problems over to his big brother to fix.

Gage wasn't stupid, though. He knew he was fully to blame for Denny's dependence on him. His fault for cutting his kid brother too much slack. But Denny wasn't as strong as him. He wouldn't have survived their childhood if Gage hadn't been around to protect him.

It hadn't come as much of a surprise when Denny grew up to be an addict. Gage's little brother was too weak to deal with real-life problems. He preferred to hide behind the high and let Gage bail him out whenever he messed up.

But Reed was right about another thing—Gage couldn't keep rescuing his brother. He might've signed up for three months' worth of bruises, cuts, and broken ribs to keep Denny out of danger, but after he paid off his brother's debt, he was done. Cutting him loose for good this time.

Un-fucking-likely. You'll never stop protecting him.

He ignored the internal accusation. Mostly because it was too depressing to dwell on.

"Anyway, I'd wish you luck for tomorrow, but we both know you don't need it." Reed looked ready to say more, but the loud buzzing of his phone interrupted the conversation. He swiped the handset off the desk and answered with a quick, "Yeah?" Then he paused, and the shit-eating grin that stretched across his face raised Gage's hackles—especially since it was directed at *him*.

"Take her up to Gage's office. He's on his way." Reed hung up, the smile widening. "Guess what, bro? You've got a visitor."

His pulse sped up at the same time an exasperated breath flew out of his mouth.

Goddamn her. He'd *told* her not to come back.

"So…it was nothing, huh?" Reed's expression conveyed sheer and total enjoyment.

Gage bit back a curse, then left the office without another word.

Chapter Three

Skyler paced the small office, already second-guessing her decision to show up tonight…until the door swung open and her nerves evaporated like a puff of steam.

The man who appeared in the doorway was even sexier than she remembered. Decked out in all black, he lingered for a beat before stepping inside and shutting the door behind him.

The closer he got, the faster her heart raced. She devoured the sight of him, the form-fitting pants hugging his long, muscular legs, the snug T-shirt molded to his sculpted chest. Her mouth ran dry when she spotted the tattoos curling out from his sleeves. No color, just black flames and curved designs inked into his tanned flesh, making him look dangerous and badass and really, *really* hot.

"Why did you come back?" A deep rasp, his eyes glimmering with equal doses of irritation and desire.

"You know why."

Skyler had never felt more brazen as she met him halfway. She didn't touch him or lean in to kiss him, but you'd think she had with the way his gaze flooded with heat.

"I meant what I said last night, Skyler—you don't need or want a man like me in your life."

So resigned, which only heightened her curiosity, her need to get to know this man. "You act like I'm here to propose marriage." She smiled faintly. "But we both know I came for something else. Gage."

His eyes narrowed. "You asked around about me."

"Actually, I Googled you."

"Yeah, and what'd you find out?" He didn't look angry, just intrigued.

"That you really do own this club. That you used to be a professional fighter. And as far as I can tell, you've never been arrested for a crime."

"I see." He slanted his head. "And that's good enough for you, huh? You're still prepared to let a total stranger fuck you? To spread your legs and let me shove my cock inside you?"

Her breath caught. "Are you always so blunt?"

"Yes."

"I…like it."

He sighed. "Figures."

Skyler had to grin. "Oh, I get it, you're trying to turn me off. You think graphic dirty talk will send me running in the other direction. Well, guess what, big guy, I'm not going anywhere."

"You're a stubborn little thing, aren't you?"

"Yep."

A muscle on his face twitched in evident frustration, much to her amusement. And God, now that her gaze was focused on his strong jaw, she wanted nothing more than to reach up and touch it.

So she did.

He jerked when her fingers swept over the dark stubble

on his chin, but he didn't push her hand away. That was a start, at least. He stood there, eyes shuttered, shoulders rigid, as she stroked his jaw, but she knew her touch affected him because his breathing had gone labored.

The bristly hair on his face scratched her fingertips. A shiver skipped through her as she imagined it scratching other parts of her body. Her neck, breasts, inner thighs. Holy hell, she couldn't *wait*.

"You were right," she murmured.

He blinked. "About what?"

"I'm not impulsive or free-spirited and I don't go around sleeping with men I've just met. I'm a good girl, okay? I'm doing my master's in psychology. I wait tables at a steakhouse on Charles Street to make rent and put myself through school. I pay my bills on time. I don't jaywalk. My grand total of past lovers is a whopping two. I'd rather stay home and watch *Top Chef* than go out." She offered a sheepish shrug. "So yes, good girl is my middle name. But…" Skyler rubbed her index finger over his bottom lip, and was rewarded by his sharp intake of breath. "But that doesn't mean I can't be bad."

"Is that really what you want?" he said roughly. "To be bad with me?"

God, yes. There was no doubt in her mind that Gage was exactly what she needed right now. He was her chance to break free of this annoying rut and let loose for a change.

"Yes, that's what I want," she answered, her tone firm. "So stop worrying about taking advantage of me, or that I'll wake up tomorrow with regrets. I *want* this."

She saw the resistance in his eyes chipping away, but wasn't surprised when he voiced one final protest. "I'm too old for you."

She mock gasped. "Oh my God. You're fifty years old. I knew it."

"Thirty," he said tersely.

"Holy shit. You're *six* years older than me?" Now she pretended to gag. "Gross. I feel violated."

"Very funny."

"Any more objections, or will you just kiss me already?"

Gage stared at her for what seemed like an eternity.

And then his mouth came crashing down on hers.

She gasped in delight, grabbing the front of his shirt and holding on for dear life. He was as dominating as she remembered, slipping his tongue between her parted lips with such skill and confidence she couldn't help but be impressed. As his tongue teased hers in a hungry circle, he shoved one hand in her hair, and suddenly she was incredibly glad she'd worn it loose. She liked the way his long fingers threaded through it, the rough pull on her scalp as he grasped the back of her head to control the kiss. His other hand traveled down her body, curling over her hip and yanking her closer to him.

It was impossible not to moan at the feel of his massive erection. She wiggled her pelvis over it, drawing a strangled groan from his lips. He tore his mouth away, breathing hard as he met her eyes. "You are goddamn addictive." His fingers dug into her hip. "You shouldn't be here."

"Well, I am, and you're not going to send me away, are you, Gage?" The taunt slipped out before she could stop it. Maybe it was the wild gleam in his eyes fueling her boldness. The desperation, the hunger. No man had ever looked at her like that before, and it made her realize just how much power she had. *She* had put that look on his face. *She* had caused that bulge in his pants.

"I would if I was smart, but I'm not," he muttered. "I'm stupid and horny and I want you too damn much." His mouth found her neck, hot and insistent as he sucked hard enough to make her gasp.

Her hands were shaking like branches in a windstorm, so she flattened them against his chest and was floored by the rock-hard mass beneath her palms. His muscles were carved out of stone, his chest so broad she felt tiny in comparison.

He kissed his way back to her mouth, capturing it in a blistering kiss that made her see stars. She registered the sensation of motion; her legs were moving somehow—no, *Gage* was moving her, backing her into the desk. She squeaked when her butt connected with something solid, and suddenly she wasn't on her feet anymore. He'd lifted her up on the desk, sinking to his knees before she could blink.

"You want to be bad?" His tone was low, dangerous, *thrilling*. "Well, you came to the right place."

She'd worn a dress again, filmy green material that hung to her knees, but now it was caught between his fingers. He slowly dragged the fabric up her legs, nostrils flaring when her bikini panties were revealed.

"Pink panties," he mumbled.

She could barely speak past the arousal tightening her throat. "Is there something wrong with that?"

He laughed harshly. "Makes perfect sense. Good-girl panties. Because you're a good girl, aren't you, Skyler?"

She swallowed. "Not tonight."

"No. Not tonight."

Callused fingers glided up her legs, leaving shivers in their wake. He swept his thumbs over her thighs, then parted her legs in one fluid, deliberate motion.

Skyler peered down at him, mesmerized. She couldn't believe she had a big, commanding man kneeling in front of her, his features taut with hunger and passion and… something else. Wonder, she realized. His gray eyes shone with wonder, like he'd discovered an unimaginable treasure he'd never expected to find.

He went motionless, palms flat on her thighs, his chest rising as he drew a breath.

"Do something," she whispered.

Slowly, his gaze met hers. "What do you want me to do?"

"Anything. Everything."

His hand moved over her thigh in an infinitesimal caress. She trembled. "Please."

He stroked his way between her legs. Circled his thumb over her clit before cupping her sex over her panties.

Her core clenched, aching so hard it hurt. She knew he'd felt how damp her panties were, because he chuckled softly. "So wet," he remarked. "Is it all for me?"

"You know it is."

Still chuckling, he pushed aside the crotch of her underwear and dipped one finger in the moisture pooling at her entrance. "*Hell.* You're wetter than I thought." She watched with wide eyes as he brought that wicked finger to his lips and sucked it, licking off her juices with a groan of approval. "And you taste as sweet as I knew you would." He popped his finger out of his mouth. "Do you want me to make you come, Skyler?"

"God. Why are you even asking?" She couldn't believe the infuriating man. She was sprawled on his desk, panting, shaking, legs wide open. Couldn't he see she was *starving* for him?

"I need to hear you say it." A command, low and seductive.

She swallowed again. "I want you to make me come."

His lips curved as he hooked his fingers under her waistband and peeled her panties off. She should have felt vulnerable with his gaze fixed on her most intimate place. But she didn't. The anticipation was too distracting, the ache too strong. She held her breath, waiting, *needing*, but he didn't move. Didn't touch her. She was seconds away from begging when he slid closer and pressed his mouth directly on her clit.

"*Oh.*"

The jolt of pleasure nearly knocked her off the desk, and she grabbed on to the edge to steady herself. Gage's mouth was hot against her sensitive flesh, the pressure of his lips almost unbearable, but then his tongue darted out and licked her so gently her eyes blinked open in surprise. She hadn't expected the tenderness. The slow, sweet glide of his tongue.

And then he did it again. And again. One leisurely, torturous lick after another, until she was squirming uncontrollably, every inch of skin tight and hot and prickling with frustration.

"I need more," she choked out.

Gage lifted his head and licked his glossy lips. "You want me to suck on your clit?"

The explicit suggestion made her moan. "*Yes*."

"You want my fingers inside you?"

Her head jerked in a nod. She knew she was broadcasting her need for release loud and clear, but Gage seemed unfazed. He actually had the nerve to grin. An evil, filthy grin that sent her heart rate into overdrive. "Pity. You're just gonna have to wait."

The gentle assault continued. The tiniest licks. The sweetest kisses. The barely there thrust of his tongue as its tip teased her opening. Sweat broke out on her forehead when he parted her folds with his fingers and nuzzled her with his cheek, releasing a groan of pure contentment that vibrated through her body. The man was killing her. *Killing* her.

She brought her hands to his head, trying to pull him closer, but his dark hair was too short to grip, and he ducked out of her hold with a smug laugh. She arched her hips next, tried to bring her pussy to his face instead, but that only earned her another burst of laughter, another teasing kiss.

"Please." The chord of desperation in her voice startled her. "Please, Gage. *Please*."

"That's it, bad girl. I just needed to hear you beg." Growling softly, he wrapped his lips around her clit and pushed two fingers inside her.

The orgasm swept through her like a flash flood. She cried out and fell back on her elbows, rocking her hips with each pulsing wave of pleasure. When his mouth and fingers abruptly disappeared, she moaned in disappointment, but he didn't leave her for long. He stood up and stepped into the cradle of her thighs, grinding his pelvis into her throbbing sex as he bent down to kiss her.

She tasted herself on his lips, which was new and foreign but didn't stop her from hungrily kissing him back. The mind-blowing release had only heightened her excitement. She wanted more. So much more. Her hands moved between them, fumbling with his belt, somehow managing to unbuckle it and unzip his pants despite her shaky fingers. They both groaned when she reached into his pants and grasped his cock.

"Fuuuuck." Gage's forehead dropped on her shoulder as he thrust into her hand. "That's it, baby. Keep doing that."

She pumped him tentatively, slightly unnerved by his size, his thickness. He was bigger than she was used to, and she couldn't wait for him to fill her. She stroked his shaft, rubbing the blunt head with her thumb on each upstroke, squeezing and fondling while she studied his expression to find out what he liked. He made a tortured noise when she quickened the pace, his hips driving forward.

"Hell, that feels fantastic." He lifted his head, a glint of humor in his eyes. "Do I even want to know how you got so damn good at giving hand jobs?"

"Practice. I'm a good girl, remember? I'm also a perfectionist. If I don't know how to do something, I won't quit until I've mastered it." She batted her eyelashes. "My last boyfriend didn't mind me practicing on him."

Gage choked out a laugh. "I'm sure he didn't."

"Wait until you experience my blow jobs…"

"Oh Jesus. I'm already close to coming and that's from your *hand*. If you bring that sexy mouth anywhere near my dick, I won't last more than a second."

"Hmmm. Right, and you're thirty, which means you'll *never* be able to get it up again. Old men only come once a night, right?"

More husky laughter escaped his mouth. It sounded almost rusty, like it was a sound he didn't make often, and she was pleased that she'd managed to get so many laughs out of him.

"Trust me, I can get it up again. But in case you forgot, we're in my office and I have a club to run, which means I'm only getting off once tonight." A cocky grin tugged his lips up. "And it's gonna be in your pussy."

A fresh jolt of arousal shot through her. Gosh, she loved his dirty talk. And the fact that they were in his office only made the whole encounter a million times dirtier. Hotter.

As anticipation once again gathered in her core, she gave his cock another leisurely stroke and said, "What are you waiting for, then?"

• • •

Gage couldn't look away from Skyler's big blue eyes. The woman had hypnotized him. With her beauty, her humor, the way she jacked his cock like a pro.

Practice, she'd said. Jesus. He would've cut off his own arm to be her sexual guinea pig.

"You sure that's what you want?" he asked, giving her one last chance to back out. "Me inside you?"

There was nothing sexier than the coy little smile that lifted her lips. "Condom," she murmured. "Inner pocket of my purse."

Nodding, he went to retrieve her khaki-colored canvas bag, unzipped the inside pocket, and found what he was looking for. As he rolled the condom on, he swept his gaze over Skyler, unable to fathom how she could possibly be real.

She was like a feast laid out just for him. Dark hair spilling over one shoulder, legs wide open, pussy swollen and glistening from the orgasm he'd just given her. He'd be lucky if he lasted five measly strokes before he shot off like a rocket.

"Something's not right," he mused.

Confusion filled her eyes. "What do you mean?"

He strode toward her and tugged on the bodice of her dress to reveal her breasts—and oh sweet Lord, she wasn't wearing a bra. His mouth turned to dust as he admired her tits. Her gorgeous fucking tits with puckered cherry-red nipples practically screaming to be sucked.

"There. Everything's just fine now." He bent his head and captured one nipple between his lips, sucking hard enough to draw a tortured moan from her throat. He flicked his tongue over the rigid bud before moving to lick the other one, chuckling when her impatient voice echoed in the air.

"For Pete's sake, get *inside* me already."

Deciding to have mercy on her, he positioned his cock between her legs and guided it to her opening. He slid inside, just an inch, and black spots promptly swam in his vision when her inner muscles tightened around him. Oh hell. She was tight. Deliciously tight.

"I haven't done this in a while," she confessed.

Gage smoothed strands of hair out of her face and planted a reassuring kiss on her lips. "I'll be gentle."

The promise got him a glare he didn't expect. "Where's the fun in that?"

Despite her grumbling, he kept going slow, working another inch into her, then another, and another. Heat surrounded his cock, and the grip of her pussy was so unbearably tight he shuddered in pleasure. He was seconds away from coming and he hadn't even started to move yet.

"I mean it, Gage, don't you dare hold back."

A curse flew out of his mouth. "I'm not holding back for you, baby. I'm doing it for *me*."

"It's okay if it's fast," she said helpfully. "I don't usually come from intercourse anyway. Not without extra stimulation."

Damned if he didn't take that as a challenge.

"Extra stimulation?" he echoed. "You mean like this?" He shoved his hand between her legs and pressed his thumb directly over her clit.

She gasped so loudly he grinned.

"Yes. Like that."

"Now be a good girl and get close again." He leaned in and kissed her neck, teasing her feverish flesh with his tongue. "I'm not moving until you're ready."

"Seriously?"

"One thing you should know about me—I don't make idle threats." He nipped the side of her jaw, continuing to strum her clit while his cock stayed lodged inside her.

Every muscle in his body strained, his brain shouting for him to move. To slide out of her tight channel and plunge back in and ease the agonizing ache in his groin. But he didn't. He refused to let go until he saw that look of ecstasy flood her eyes again. Until he watched her come apart in his arms and heard her scream his name.

"You're just torturing yourself," she wheezed out. "It will take me longer to come the second time."

"Maybe, but it'll be worth the wait." He drew lazy circles over her clit, watching her face as he teased the swollen bud. When her eyelids fluttered closed, he grasped her chin with his free hand. "Look at me, Skyler. Watch me as I get you off."

Her eyes popped open, cheeks flushed and lips parted as she focused on him.

He applied more pressure on her clit, heard her answering moan, and decided he deserved a goddamn medal for his restraint. Any other man might have given in. Thrown control into the wind and screwed her brains out, but he didn't move an inch. Beads of sweat rose on his forehead, his dick aching so bad it was starting to get seriously painful.

He suddenly saw stars when Skyler abruptly rocked into him.

"No," he commanded, grasping her hip to keep her still. "You don't move until I tell you to. You're going to sit there like the good girl you are while I play with you."

Her breathing grew more unstable by the moment. "You're so evil."

"You love it, baby."

"I do," she moaned. "I really do."

Chuckling, he continued to work her clit with fingers.

Waited. Watched.

Gage had no clue how much time passed. Several minutes at least. Long enough that his balls drew up in agony, his cock screaming for release, for friction, for anything.

"I…oh…I'm almost there." Desperation creased her face. "Oh, Gage. *Now*."

Thank God.

His hips shot back like a cannonball, then thrust forward with so much force it knocked the computer keyboard right off the desk. He slammed into her hard, groaning when he felt her pussy spasm around his cock. Every sense came alive, pleasure prickling over his skin, surging through his blood. Three more thrusts and he came as violently as she was, panting for air as the orgasm sizzled through his body in hot, pulsing waves.

It took a while to crash back to earth. His hands shook as he cupped her face. "You good, baby?"

She nodded wordlessly, eyes hazy with satisfaction.

Christ, he wanted to stay inside her forever, and it was with extreme reluctance that he withdrew from her tight sheath. Skyler straightened her dress while he disposed of the condom, and as he zipped up his pants, he noticed the displeased frown marring her lips.

"I didn't get to see you naked." She pouted. "I *really* wanted to see you naked."

He laughed hoarsely. "I'm sorry?"

She slid off the desk and marched right into his personal space, leaning up to kiss him before speaking in a firm voice. "We're going to see each other again, by the way."

Wariness rose in his throat. "Skyler…"

"I intended for tonight to be a onetime thing, but I've changed my mind. This was way too good not to do again."

He couldn't argue with her there. Hands down, the best sex of his life.

But it hadn't changed his mind, either. His life was too screwed up, too damn dark. Skyler, on the other hand…she radiated light and goodness. He refused to drag her down with him.

Besides, even if he didn't have a shit-ton of headaches on his plate right now, he still wouldn't be able to give her what she needed. What every woman needed.

He'd figured out a long time ago that he sucked at relationships. Too many of his exes had accused him of being a cold bastard, and who could forget his last serious relationship four years ago, when Lisa had burst into tears and wailed about how she wanted him to *need* her. She'd insisted that he held a part of himself back, refused to lean on her or accept her support, and he supposed there was some truth to that.

Gage had never been able to rely on a single person in his life, except for his mom, who'd died when he was too damn young. After her death, he'd been truly alone, forced to take care not only of himself, but of his kid brother. At fourteen he'd worked two after-school jobs to pay the rent because his old man spent all their money on alcohol. He'd relied on *himself*, the only person he trusted to get shit done.

So yeah, he didn't need anyone, not when he was perfectly capable of going at it alone, but none of the women he'd dated seemed to understand or accept that.

Gage opened his mouth, but Skyler silenced him with another fleeting kiss. "Don't you dare tell me it won't happen again. Because it will."

Indecision flashed through him.

"Look me in the eye and tell me you don't want to have sex with me again," she challenged.

A groan slipped out. "God. Of course I do. But…"

"But nothing. You can't deprive either one of us of something this good. It would be a grave injustice."

His lips twitched in a smile, and damn it, but he could feel his resolve crumbling. "If we see each other again—"

"*When* we see each other again."

"*Before* we do," he corrected, "we need to lay down a few ground rules."

"What kind of rules?"

"Actually, there's only one. This thing between us…it'll just be sex. That's all I can give you."

"Fine, great, I'll take six more orgasms." She blinked. "Wait, that number is too low. I'll take…twenty?"

His lips twitched. "I'm being serious. I'm not looking for a relationship—I want to be clear about that right off the bat."

"Gotcha. Sex only." She went back to the desk, found a notepad and pen, and quickly scribbled something down. "That's my number. I'm leaving it right here on your desk." She found her purse and promptly pulled out her phone. "What's yours?"

Gage hesitated.

"If you don't give it to me yourself, I'll just get it some other way. I'm very resourceful."

A sigh escaped. "Yeah, I bet you are," he said, before reciting his digits.

She punched the number in with a broad smile. "There. Was that so hard?" She tucked her cell back in her purse. "Okay, I'm going now. You're at work, and I don't want to keep you."

Before Skyler could move for the door, he grabbed her arm and pulled her toward him, his mouth capturing hers in a kiss that left her wide-eyed and breathless.

"Do you need me to call you a cab?" he said roughly.

She looked touched. "No, that's okay. I drove." There was a beat. "PS—if I don't hear from you in a reasonable amount of time, I'm calling you myself. Got it?"

Gage fought hard not to grin. Shit, he really liked her. The no-nonsense attitude, the confidence.

God help him, but he really did want to see her again.

"Got it," he said dutifully.

Chapter Four

"Sex," Lacey said the next morning, her skeptical tone revealing her exact thoughts on the matter.

Skyler nodded.

"*Just* sex."

"Yep. Just sex." She popped the last bite of fruit salad in her mouth as she awaited a response.

From the moment she'd gotten home last night, Skyler had been dying to tell her friends about her visit to Gage, but since they were never around, she'd had no choice but to go to them. May was too busy at the museum to sneak away for a chat, but luckily Lacey had been able to squeeze in a quick breakfast in the hospital cafeteria.

"I give you a week," Lacey finally said. "Actually, forget that. I give you a *weekend*."

Skyler furrowed her brow. "Before what?"

"Before you either (a) break it off with him because sex isn't enough, or (b) convince him to officially date you because sex isn't enough. Common denominator? Sex won't be enough." With a smug look, Lacey sipped her coffee and watched Skyler over the rim of her cup.

"That's not necessarily true," she protested. "I'm really liking this arrangement so far."

"You only hooked up once!" Lacey said with a laugh. "Twice if you count that first night. *Of course* you like it now. It's new and exciting and who has time for conversations with a guy when you're too busy sexing him up? But once the shine wears off and the sex stops being oh-my-God-new, you'll want to get to know him. Suddenly you're asking him questions like *where did you grow up* and *what's your deepest, darkest fear?* And before long it'll be *take me to the farmers' market, Gage,* or *let's go on a picnic!* And then bam! You've fallen for him and now you're in a relationship." Lacey's tone softened. "Or even worse, you fall for him and he breaks your heart."

"I don't think that will happen. I mean, he's not my usual type at all. I think that's why it's so exciting, you know?" Skyler absently traced the edge of her coffee cup with her index finger. "But he's not someone I picture myself with in the long run."

"Right. I forgot. Because you're more interested in men of the boring and stable variety," Lacey teased.

She stuck out her tongue, which was pretty much the only suitable response considering her friend was absolutely right. Skyler had only had two long-term relationships in her life, both with nice, dependable guys who, depressing as it was to admit, really had been kind of boring.

And yet given the choice, she'd still pick dependable and boring over wild and exciting any day. Wild and exciting didn't pay the bills, or keep a roof over your head, or raise children with you.

She couldn't deny that Gage made her heart pound like no man ever had, but she didn't know much about him except that he was rough around the edges and owned a nightclub. It was way too premature to think about any sort of future with the guy.

"We'll see what happens," she said with a shrug. "Right now, I'm not thinking past the out-of-this-world sex." She grinned. "Aren't you even a teeny bit happy that I'm having fun for a change?"

"Oh, for sure," Lacey answered. "I was starting to worry about you. Seriously. It's not normal for someone as young and hot as you to not have a life."

Skyler snickered. She gestured around the cafeteria, then at Lacey's bright pink scrubs. "Look who's talking. You practically live at this hospital."

"Babe, you've seen *Grey's Anatomy*—there's a lot more than medicine and life-saving going on around here." With a wink, the brunette nodded toward the buffet line. "For example. See that fine-assed man over there?"

Skyler followed her friend's gaze, raising a brow when she noticed the incredibly handsome blond. "Yeah?" She turned back with a knowing look.

"Oh yeah. Dr. Josh Lewis. We have regularly scheduled hookup sessions in the on-call lounge." Lacey wiggled her eyebrows. "Trust me. I most certainly have a life. A very, very active one."

Skyler's phone buzzed, putting a halt to the conversation. When she glanced at the screen, a frown immediately puckered her lips.

Her friend snorted. "Trouble in just-sex-paradise already?"

"Naah, it's not Gage." She paused. "Clay."

Lacey's expression went serious. "What does he want?"

Skyler skimmed the message again, then stifled a sigh. "Same old. Just to see how I'm doing and ask if I want to pop in for dinner this week."

"Let me guess, you'll reply with your usual I'm-too-busy bullshit."

She shrugged, fighting her rising discomfort. Which only

got worse when she noticed the disapproval glittering in her friend's brown eyes.

"What?" she said defensively.

After a beat, Lacey shook her head. "Nothing. I just feel sorry for him sometimes. He's trying so hard."

The uncomfortable feeling transformed into a knot of guilt. It was true—her stepfather really did make an effort to reach out to her. No matter how many times she blew him off, he still kept calling, texting, and emailing every few weeks. Like clockwork.

But his attempts to connect with her only seemed to make Skyler withdraw even more. It didn't matter how many years had passed, or how hard she tried to move past it—she still viewed Clay Rivers as the man who'd broken up her parents' marriage, and being around him was just a bleak reminder of her mom's betrayal and her dad's heartache.

"I'm a real hypocrite, huh?" Skyler let out a heavy breath. "Here I am, studying to become a therapist, and yet I totally refuse to deal with my own issues. In my head I know Clay's not fully to blame for everything that happened, but every time I see him, I can't help but feel it."

"I know, babe. Your whole life was turned upside down because of him. But…" Lacey sighed too. "Eventually you'll have to make a decision. Whether to deal with this Clay stuff head-on, or just cut him off completely."

"Eventually," she echoed, keeping her tone light. She took a last sip of coffee before pushing her chair back. "All right. I've gotta hit the library. I still need to finish up my conclusion for that abuse victims paper."

"Any big plans for tonight?" Lacey grinned as they picked up their trays and headed for the row of trash cans across the cafeteria.

"Probably not. I haven't heard from Gage."

"Well, I hope you do. You need to make the most of the

sexy times while they're still deliciously new." Lacey put on a strict face. "But remember—don't fall in love with him."

Skyler rolled her eyes. "I'll try not to."

. . .

The warehouse was filled to the rafters. Gage swallowed a tired sigh as he maneuvered through the throng of people, wishing he were anywhere but here. The crowd was more boisterous than usual, releasing cheers, jeers, and deafening screams as the two fighters in the cage beat the crap out of each other. And the air was sweltering hot, thanks to the hundreds of bodies crammed in the large space. He was already sweating, and he hadn't even gotten in the cage yet.

He ignored the wave of hellos and back slaps he encountered on his way to the roped-off area on one side of the room, where three rows of "elite" seats offered an unobstructed view of the cage. Several shady characters occupied the VIP seats, although on paper, everything about the arena was legal. Permits, liquor licenses, vendors—all aboveboard. And yet there was nothing aboveboard about the man who ran the fights.

Mitch O'Donnell rose at Gage's approach, looking pleased as punch to see him. He was a big man, six five to Gage's six two, but lanky rather than built. He had pale skin and red hair tied back in a ponytail, and an unlit cigar dangling from the corner of his mouth. "Glad you made it, Holt."

He said it as if Gage actually had a *choice* in the matter.

"Any instructions for tonight?" he asked after he'd nodded in greeting.

Mitch raised one reddish eyebrow, waiting for clarification.

"Do you want me to win or lose?" Gage said in a curt voice.

The other man looked annoyed. "Why the hell do you

gotta ask me that every time? Have I ever ordered you to throw a fight?"

Gage shrugged.

"You know what I want, brother. Beat the shit outta your opponent and make us some goddamn money."

"Gotcha." He had to admit, he thoroughly enjoyed seeing the aggravation clouding the other man's eyes. Gage always made a point to inquire whether he should throw the fight, just because he knew that the implication that Mitch fixed matches pissed the guy off. He also knew it was the truth—more often than not, Mitch *did* arrange the outcome of the fights.

But Gage had never lost or thrown a match. Not once during his professional days, and not once in the seven fights he'd already given Mitch.

"How's my man Denny doing these days?" Mitch asked.

His shoulders stiffened. "He's good. Clean as a whistle."

"Good. Good for him." The man clucked his tongue. "It was such a bloody shame, seeing him fall off the wagon again."

"I bet it was," Gage murmured, not believing a word of it.

Mitch had relished having Denny under his thumb. Dealing drugs for him, doing his dirty work in Southie. The bastard had probably come in his pants after Denny's royal screw up, because now he had Denny's big brother under his thumb, too.

"Tell him to stop by and see me one of these days," Mitch said. "I know he's out of the drug business, but we're still buds, no?"

"Sure, I'll tell him." Yeah, fucking right.

A bone-jarring crunch had them both cocking their heads at the cage in time to see one of the fighters stumble backward, fist pressed to his nose as blood poured down his chin.

"Damn right!" Mitch shouted, clapping his hands in delight. "That's it, Colin! Show that mofo who's boss!"

"I'll find you after the match," Gage muttered, edging away from O'Donnell.

He stalked toward the locker rooms, desperate for some peace and quiet. It didn't take him long to get ready. He was already wearing his boxing shorts, so all he had to do was strip off his hoodie and wifebeater, kick off his sneakers, and he was almost ready to go.

He sank onto the splintered wooden bench and taped up his hands, grateful that nobody was around to chat him up. Christ. He was so sick of this shit. He'd quit fighting for a reason: because he was *tired*. Tired of walking around black-and-blue all the time, tired of the ache in his bones. His nose had been broken so many times it was a miracle it'd stayed on his face, and he'd dealt with so many fractured ribs he was surprised he'd never punctured a lung.

Three more.

He took a breath, clinging to the reminder. Three more matches, and he and Mitch would be square, Mitch and Denny would be square. And he had a good thing going over at Sin. The club had turned a profit in its first year of business, which meant he had a ton of cash in his bank account. He didn't need to fight anymore. He didn't *want* to fight anymore.

He wasn't sure how long he sat in the locker room. Other men wandered in and out, changing into fighter gear, shooting the shit with each other, but Gage just sat there, shoulders tense, gaze downcast, until a male voice finally called his name from the doorway.

"Holt, you're up." One of Mitch's people entered the locker room. LeSean something or other.

Gage got to his feet. "Who am I facing?"

The beefy black man actually cracked a smile, something Gage had never seen him do. "Robbie O'Reilly."

He blew out a curse. "Seriously? That crazy fucker from Dorchester? Why does he keep coming back?"

At least it made sense now, why Mitch had looked so annoyed at the thought of Gage losing. Mitch was no doubt eager for him to kick O'Reilly's ass like he'd done last month. During their previous meeting, O'Reilly had fought so dirty Gage had no choice but to go apeshit on him, and the results had been a damn bloodbath.

"I guess he likes getting his ass whupped," LeSean answered. "Watch yourself out there, white boy. I saw O'Reilly fight at that gym in Roxbury last week and it looks like he's added biting to his li'l bag of tricks."

"Wonderful."

LeSean clapped him on the back. "Don't sweat it. You'll tap him out."

Yeah, but how bad of a beating would he take before that happened?

Chapter Five

Skyler's cell phone rang just past midnight. She'd been watching a *Top Chef* marathon in bed, so she was fully alert as she reached for the phone. Her heart jumped when she glimpsed Gage's number on the screen, and she wasted no time picking up with a quick, "Hello?"

"Hey." His deep voice slid into her ear and rippled through her body. "Can I see you tonight?"

Wow. Okay. She hadn't expected to hear from him tonight, and she frowned when she glanced at the clock on the bedside table. In her very limited experience, anything after 11 p.m. equaled a booty call. That was just Sex Etiquette 101.

On the other hand, hadn't they agreed this arrangement was 100 percent sex-centered?

On the other *other* hand, just because she'd agreed to a casual fling didn't mean midnight booty calls were okay. Did she really want to give him the impression that he could call her at any hour of the day and she'd be like, *Sure! Come over and fuck me!*

Except…the word *no* got stuck in her mouth. Because

darn it, she *wanted* him to come over and fuck her.

Gage must have sensed her internal dilemma because he laughed softly. "I know it's late, but I just finished…work." The stilted pause between the words raised her guard, but he hurried on before she could question it. "I would've called earlier if I could. But if you're too tired or don't feel like it, then that's fine. We can just see each other another ti—"

"Would you just get here already?" she interrupted.

Oh boy. Her voice sounded breathy to her ears. She had it *bad*.

"What's the address?" He paused as she recited it, then said, "I'm on my way."

Skyler flew out of bed the second he hung up, self-consciously examining her bedroom. It was messier than usual, which prompted her to run around like a madwoman in an attempt to tidy up. Thank God her room was on the third floor and had its own private bath—if she'd shared a floor with Lacey and May, they might have witnessed her cleaning frenzy and teased her mercilessly about it.

Luckily, her roommates weren't even home tonight. Lacey was still at the hospital, and May had left a note on the fridge about spending the night at her boyfriend's.

She and Gage would be completely alone.

Nervous excitement scampered down her body and flew into her stomach in the form of butterflies. She was dying to see him again, but at the same time, she wasn't sure why she was so taken with the guy. He was a man who'd once made his living with his fists, who now owned a club called Sin. *Sin*, of all things.

The only sin she'd ever committed was…well, having sex in a nightclub with a man she barely knew. Unless smoking pot qualified as sinful—she'd done a bunch of that during freshman year when the stress of college had gotten too overwhelming.

Damn, girl, you're so *wild.*

Skyler laughed out loud. Yep, she sure was wild—it was Saturday night and she was at home watching a cooking competition on TV.

No, it's Saturday night and you're about to have a sexy late-night visitor.

Hmmm. Fair point. Maybe she was broadening her wild horizons, after all.

It felt like an eternity before the doorbell finally rang, though in reality, only ten minutes had passed since Gage's call.

The first thing she did after she'd opened the door was gasp. "Oh my God! What happened?"

Genuine confusion filled Gage's expression. "What are you talking about?"

She touched his face without thinking, and he winced when her fingers skimmed the bruise marring his left cheekbone. "Oh, right. That. Don't worry about it. Just a bruise."

"Did you get in a fight?" Her concern levels remained on high as she grabbed his hand and ushered him into the living room.

He spared a glance at his surroundings, unfazed by the sparse amount of furniture. "I fought in a match tonight." He shrugged. "My opponent was kind of a dick."

She furrowed her eyebrows. "I thought you retired."

"Not really." He didn't offer any more details.

Jeez. She'd probably have better luck extracting answers from a CIA operative.

"You're wearing pink again."

The gruff observation made her grin. "Sharp as a tack, aren't you, big guy?"

Amusement twinkled in his gray eyes, but they darkened seductively as he examined her pink tank top and matching boxer shorts. "I've never hung out with a girl in pink PJs before."

"No? What do the women you know usually wear to bed?"

He smirked. "Nothing at all."

"They're lucky, then. I can't sleep naked. My butt and boobs get too cold."

Gage barked out a laugh, then stepped forward and pulled her in for a kiss.

Shock waves hit her the moment their lips met. God, she loved kissing him. Loved that he didn't try to drown her in saliva or gnash her with his teeth. Everything he did was deliberate and skillful, from the firm press of his lips to the sensual swirl of his tongue. She moaned against his mouth, sucking on his bottom lip as heat spread through her and settled in her core.

"Fuck." He jerked them apart. "Bedroom?"

"Upstairs." Smiling impishly, she moved toward the doorway. "Coming?"

The predatory gleam in his eyes sparked a flurry of shivers. He followed her to the hall, his muscular frame towering over her. The man radiated pure power and potent masculinity, and the bruise on his face only added to the dangerous vibes he was emitting.

They didn't speak as they climbed the stairs. Skyler felt his breath tickling the nape of her neck, but he didn't touch her, not even when they entered her bedroom. Though they were alone in the house, she still closed the door out of habit, and then sank down on the edge of the mattress.

Gage didn't join her. He lingered at the foot of the bed, his smoky eyes containing a hint of hesitation, as if he was waiting for her to direct him.

"Take off your clothes," she told him.

The corners of his mouth crinkled in a smile. "You really want to see me naked, huh?"

"I'm dying to." She flashed him her sweetest look. "Pretty please?"

She half expected him to make her beg—he seemed to enjoy doing that—but before she could blink, he pulled his hoodie right over his head. That left him in a wifebeater and jeans, though it didn't take long for those to disappear too, right along with his sneakers, socks, and boxers.

Her jaw dropped as sleek golden skin and sculpted muscles assaulted her vision. His body was incredible, long limbs and hard sinew and not a single ounce of fat anywhere on him. Her gaze lowered to his cock, which jutted out enticingly, so long and thick it made her heart pound, the loud drumming drowning out the sound of the TV.

"You shouldn't be allowed to wear clothes," she sputtered. "I'm serious. There needs to be a law against it."

He chuckled. "You're liable to give me an ego."

"You're liable to make me come just from looking at you."

"That's the nicest thing anyone's ever said to me, baby." His hand drifted down his chest, palm splaying over his rippled abs, perilously close to his cock. "Now what? You want me to stand here naked? Put on a show for you?"

A strangled sound escaped her lips.

"Oh yeah. You like that idea." Smirking, he curled his large fist around his erection and gave it a slow pump.

Heat suffused Skyler's body. God, was this actually happening? Was she seriously watching the sexiest man in the world touch himself in front of her?

Yep, she was, because no way did she have the kind of dirty imagination required to make something like this up.

Her gaze followed the erotic movement of his hand, noting the way he squeezed the head of his cock on each upward stroke, the rough grip he kept around his shaft.

"Can I…" Her throat bobbed in a desperate swallow,

mouth so dry it was like talking through a wad of sand. "Can I suck your cock?"

A groan ripped out of his throat.

"Is that a yes?"

"C'mere," he growled.

She slid off the bed and scrambled to her knees in front of him. Her mouth wasn't dry anymore. It had filled with moisture, lips tingling with anticipation as she rested both hands on his muscular thighs. The wiry hairs there tickled her palms, and his erection seemed to thicken right before her eyes, a pearly drop forming at the tip.

Shivering, she leaned in and swiped her tongue over his engorged head.

His whole body shuddered from the tiny, barely there lick. "I don't deserve this," he mumbled.

Her brow furrowed as she looked up at him. "What do you mean?"

"An hour ago I was beating the crap out of some guy, and now the most beautiful woman I've ever met is on her knees about to suck me off. It doesn't seem right."

"Stop being so melodramatic," she chided.

"Skyler—"

She didn't let him finish. She simply took his cock in her mouth and sucked all the way down to the root.

Gage jerked as if he'd been shot. "Oh fuck. Oh *hell*. That feels so good."

Laughing, she released him with a *pop*, then explored his shaft with her tongue, licking and tasting and memorizing every inch of him. Her lazy exploration drew tortured noises from him, so she began alternating between soft licks followed by tight suction, until his hands tangled in her hair and his hips moved in a restless rhythm.

"You were right," he choked out. "This is even better than your hand job."

She smiled, then swiped her tongue around his head in teasing circles. The floor beneath her knees was cold, but she barely noticed because flames had engulfed her body and turned her into a hot mess. Her nipples tightened painfully, sex tingling as pressure coiled inside her. She loved the taste of him, the way his cock throbbed against her tongue and filled her mouth.

Her gag reflex was nonexistent, which made it possible to scarf down the inedible food her roommates prepared—and made it easy to swallow Gage's cock effortlessly until his tip hit the back of her throat. She sucked hard and fast, relishing the husky sounds that left his mouth and heated the air.

"Jesus, did you take a fucking workshop on deep-throating?" Agony and pleasure mingled in his voice. When she looked up, his features were stretched taut, eyes glittering with pleasure.

All she could do was smile again, a rush of female satisfaction coursing through her veins. He was getting close. She heard it in his labored breathing, felt it in the erratic thrust of his hips. She couldn't wait to taste him, but he didn't give her the chance. With a low groan, he pulled her up by the hair, then grinned when her disappointed grumble echoed between them.

"Look at that sad face," he teased. "You like sucking my dick that much, huh?"

"Mmm-hmm, and you're a jerk for taking it away from me."

The accusation didn't faze him. He was too busy leading her to the bed, hurriedly tugging at her pajamas before curling his body over hers until she lay on the mattress, flat on her back with his heavy chest crushing her bare breasts.

"Maybe, but I'm giving you something in return," he rasped, then inched lower and closed his mouth over her nipple.

Skyler's hips shot off the bed. When he gently bit the sensitive bud, the sensation was so intense she cried out and clasped her hands on his head, begging for more.

"These are the prettiest tits I've ever seen." His hot breath fanned over her tingling flesh. "I never want to stop playing with them."

God, she didn't *want* him to stop. Everything he did to her was pure heaven. The deep pulls on her nipples, the roughness of his hands as he stroked and squeezed her breasts. He moved one hand between her thighs, callused fingers seeking her clit, finding it, and rubbing so expertly her vision became hazy.

"You gonna come for me if I keep doing this?"

She rocked wildly into his hand, but it wasn't enough. "No," she wheezed. "I need more than your hand."

"Do you want my mouth?" He peered down at her with heavy-lidded eyes, painting the most appealing sight. The bruise on his cheek, the dark stubble slashing his jaw, the nose that had clearly been broken more than once—every yummy detail combined to create a sexy, masculine package that thrilled her to the core.

"No," she blurted out, the pressure too painful to handle. "I want your cock. I want you inside me while you touch my clit. The way you did yesterday."

His mouth found hers in a hot kiss, that wicked tongue doing the most amazing things to hers. Skyler couldn't breathe. She'd forgotten how. Gage had reduced her entire world to one thing—*need*. She *needed* him, damn it.

"Don't. Move." He uttered the husky command as he went to get a condom, returning to the bed a moment later, fully sheathed.

Anticipation rippled through her. She parted her legs in a blatant invitation, but he didn't take it. Instead, he stretched out on his back beside her, hooded eyes locking with hers. "Ride me," he ordered.

He didn't have to ask her twice. Skyler's pulse raced as she climbed on top of his long, sleek body. A fighter's body with the scars to prove it, though she was careful not to jostle his torso when she glimpsed another bruise forming beneath his rib cage.

His tattoos fascinated her. Neither of the guys she'd slept with had been tattooed, and if she'd known how frickin' hot an inked man was, she would've started stalking tattoo parlors years ago. But this time it wasn't the intricate flames on his biceps that captured her attention, but the set of initials above his left pectoral.

S.J.H.

She wanted to ask him what the letters stood for, but now wasn't the time. Not when she was dripping wet and his cock was standing upright, waiting for her to ride it.

"Don't be shy, baby," he taunted. "Sit on my dick."

She swallowed hard, too turned on to move, which was damn ironic because the only way to ease the ache *was* to move.

"C'mon, bad girl, what are you waiting for? I was wrestling with a sweaty dude before I got here, and sinking into your hot pussy is my reward. Give it to me."

She slammed down on his cock, then collapsed on his chest. "You say the filthiest things," she moaned.

His warm lips grazed her cheek. "That's 'cause I'm a filthy boy. A very filthy boy who needs to be punished. So now ride me until I can't see straight."

Sitting up took a serious amount of effort; she was trembling too hard. She laid her hands flat on his tight abdomen, needing an anchor, something solid to hold on to. She rose up and sank down again, her inner muscles clamping around his shaft as pleasure bolted through her.

"Why does it feel so good?" she whispered. "I've never felt anything like this before."

"Me neither," he said hoarsely.

Something hot and sweet and unfamiliar sizzled between them. A sense of connection, maybe. She tried to cling to the feeling, but Gage's fingers had found her clit again and the sensation of dizzying pleasure distracted her.

"Come on, baby," he muttered. "Make us feel even better."

The knot of urgency snapped like a bungee cord, propelling Skyler into a frenzied rhythm that left her breathless. Her hair flew in her face as she bounced on his cock, over and over again, until the pressure became too much, the arousal too painful, sending her falling against him again. She moaned with each flick of his fingers on her clit, and eventually stopped moving altogether and let him take over.

He thrust upward, hard and merciless, his rugged features straining as his chest rose and fell rapidly. Fast, deep thrusts, filling her again and again until she came in a blinding rush of bliss. Gage wasn't far behind. As he groaned in release, he held her so tightly she could barely draw a breath.

Once the pleasure abated, they lay there in silence, his large hands stroking her back, his breath tickling her forehead. Then, with a pained look, he gently eased her off him and left the bed to dispose of the condom.

He was back a moment later, sliding in behind her. One muscular arm wrapped around her to pull her flush against his body, and she practically melted into him, wiggling her bare butt until she found a comfortable position. She became aware of the voices murmuring on the TV, but she was too sated and drowsy to pay much attention. And still very naked, she realized.

"I should find my PJs," she mumbled.

Gage tightened his hold on her. "Don't worry, I'll keep you warm."

He wasn't lying. His body was like a furnace, making

her feel warm and safe and utterly contented. The first night they'd met, she never would have dreamed she'd be snuggling in bed with this man, and yet…here they were.

"He's using too much garlic."

Skyler pried her eyes open. She hadn't realized she'd closed them. "Hmmm?"

"The dude on TV. He put too much garlic in that dish."

A soft laugh slipped out. "Yeah? You think you know better than a professional chef, is that it?"

But then to her sheer amazement, after the judges tasted the chef's dish, all three of them staunchly declared that waaaaay too much garlic had been used.

"I told you." Gage's smug voice heated the back of her neck.

"Fine, clearly you *do* know better." She paused, then gave in to the spark of curiosity. "Do you like to cook?"

"I don't mind it, I guess."

"What else do you like to do? You know, in your free time?"

"I read."

She twisted her head and grinned at him. "Your monosyllabic responses are adorable. Okay. What kind of stuff do you read?"

"Fantasy. Sci-fi. Some true crime." He sounded so completely unenthused about the conversation that she wasn't surprised when he turned the tables on her. "What do *you* like to do?"

"Uh-uh. We're not discussing me right now. In case you haven't figured it out, I'm trying to get to know you better."

His heavy sigh echoed behind her. "I don't like talking. Especially about myself."

The wave of laughter that hit her would have knocked her off her feet if she hadn't been lying down. "Are you *kidding* me? When we're having sex, you talk so much you could script an entire porno movie." The giggles kept coming, until she had to curl into herself to ease the stitch in her side.

"Sex talk has nothing to do with *me*. It's about all the dirty things I want to do to *you*." His defensive grumble only made her laugh harder.

"Uh-huh, whatever you say." Her eyelids started to droop again, probably because the heat of his body made her feel like she'd stepped into a sauna. "Gosh, I'm really sleepy."

His palm grazed her hip before settling on her belly. "Go to sleep then."

She snuggled closer and tucked her feet between his, cocooned in his warmth. She was just drifting off when she felt him trying to slip away.

"This was a bad idea." Uneasiness clung to his voice. "I should go."

She answered in a fierce whisper. "Don't you dare. I'm too warm and cozy. You can't leave."

After a beat of silence, he smoothed his hand over her hair. "All right. I won't."

Skyler gave a little sigh of satisfaction and closed her eyes again.

When she woke up the next morning, Gage was gone.

Chapter Six

"You know what sucks about saying *I told you so*? You don't even get to enjoy it! I mean, you're *right* about something, which means you should be stoked, but at the same time, it means having to see your BFF bummed out, and that's no fun at all." May blew a strand of blond hair out of her eyes while maintaining an awkward-looking downward dog.

On her bright pink yoga mat, Skyler held the same pose, but craned her head to look at her friend. "You don't get to say *I told you so* yet. Not until I know for sure if it's over."

"He's been avoiding you for a week," Lacey grumbled from the neighboring mat. "I think that means it's over."

On the television screen, the perky blond yoga instructor finally broke the position and hopped to her feet. All three women sighed in relief and followed suit.

Lacey had found the *Yoga for Beginners* DVD in a grocery-store bargain bin, and after months of putting it off, the three roommates had finally found the time to watch it. Being on her feet at the restaurant every night and walking across campus on a daily basis, Skyler got enough of a workout, but she'd promised her friends she'd try yoga, and now they were holding her to it.

Didn't mean she had to enjoy it, though. Because she wasn't, not in the slightest. Yoga was *hard*. And it was too slow and motionless, which made it difficult to expend all her pent-up energy. She'd much rather run her frustrations off on a treadmill.

God, it wasn't *really* over with Gage, was it?

Sure, he hadn't responded to the three texts and two voicemails she'd left him, but maybe he was just…busy.

Oh, you silly, pathetic girl. Face the facts.

She bit her lip and moved her gaze back to the TV, hoping the next pose would distract her from the rush of disappointment that flooded her belly. It didn't. Nope, her mind stayed focused on the intense, sexy man who'd rocked her world and then disappeared like Houdini from her life.

"I don't know…I just don't get it," she blurted out. "I *know* he was into me."

"You sure about that?" Lacey asked in a careful tone.

Skyler thought about the urgency of Gage's kisses, his rough touch, the way his eyes burned when he'd moved inside her. Then she nodded. "I know it." Her teeth dug into her lip again. "I think I scared him off by asking him about his life. I was trying to get to know him and—"

"Aha!" Lacey cut in triumphantly. "I told you you'd end up doing that! See? No-strings sex is impossible."

"I guess it is," she said glumly.

"Guys, mountain pose!" May chided. "You're falling behind."

Skyler and Lacey quickly refocused their attention on the yoga at hand. For the next five minutes, they dutifully followed instructions, but it was obvious none of them had a clue what they were doing.

"Now we're going to transition into the pigeon pose," the

female instructor said serenely.

"I don't know what that is!" Lacey yelled at the TV. "Why don't you ever explain it to us?"

With that, yoga was over.

As a wave of laughter overtook her, Skyler collapsed on her back and waved her hand in surrender. "Screw this. I hate it. Let's just buy a treadmill."

"Deal," Lacey chimed in.

"Yeah, I don't have the discipline for yoga," May grumbled. "Treadmill it is."

Lacey shut off the TV, then flopped on the couch and glanced at the others. "You guys wanna order takeout and watch a movie or something?"

May was quick to nod, but Skyler hesitated.

"Uh-uh," Lacey said instantly, wagging a finger. "You can't go see him."

"But I need closure," she protested.

May sighed. "So you want to get dumped in person? Is that it?"

"If that's what it takes, then yes." Skyler undid her ponytail and ran her fingers through her hair. "I just want to know why he changed his mind, okay?"

She didn't miss the concerned look her roommates exchanged. "What?" she muttered.

"Is this guy really worth it?" May asked in a gentle voice.

Skyler swallowed. She pictured Gage's deep gray eyes, trying to pinpoint exactly what it was about him that fascinated her so damn much. What drew her to him like a moth to a flame. The night they'd met he'd told her she was playing with fire, acted like he was some scary, dangerous monster who would burn her alive.

But she wasn't afraid of him, and she didn't sense a lick of danger coming from him. If anything, his intensity only fueled the attraction.

It might have started out as a desperate need for change, for *fun*, but spending time with Gage had turned into something more than simply stepping out of her tedious rut. She liked the bold, confident woman she was when he was around, and she wasn't ready to stop exploring that part of herself yet.

"Sky?" Lacey prompted. "So is he worth it?"

She exhaled in a slow rush. "I guess I'll find out tonight."

. . .

"If I catch one more motherfucker snorting coke in the bathroom, I'm going to lose my shit," Gage snapped as he stormed into Reed's office.

Two sets of eyebrows shot up, accompanied by a low curse of amazement from AJ. "Jeez. What the hell is up *your* ass?"

Gage scowled at his friends and made a beeline for the mini-fridge in the corner of the office. He yanked open the door and grabbed a beer, angrily twisting off the cap.

"And now you're drinking on the job?" Reed piped up, equally astonished. "Seriously, man. What's going on?"

"Nothing," he mumbled.

Everything, a voice corrected.

Fine, not everything. Just one thing. One person.

Skyler.

He hadn't seen her in a week. One very long, very frustrating week, and the ironic part? It was *his* doing. *He* was the one avoiding her calls and texts.

Not that she was flooding his inbox with please-please-call-me requests. Her messages had sounded more concerned than desperate, and Gage knew he was a bona fide ass for ignoring her. But damn it, what else was he supposed to do? He was too jaded and messed up for someone like her. Skyler was sweet and funny and unbelievably *good*. She practically radiated sunshine.

And he was terrified his darkness would dim all of that incredible light. Or worse, extinguish it completely.

Sometimes he wished he were a different man. An easygoing, worry-free dude who could open up to people, trust them, lean on them, but he wasn't. He was closed off and prickly and a total bastard at times, and Skyler deserved better than that.

Lord, she made him want to be that man, though. She made him feel things no other woman ever had, and the thought of disappointing her—or worse, *hurting* her—tore at his insides like a dull razor blade. Better to cut ties now before either one of them got too close.

Only it seemed he'd underestimated the woman's tenacity.

No sooner had he taken a swig of beer than a knock came on the door, and suddenly Skyler marched into the office unannounced.

Gage's heart leaped the moment he saw her. She was wearing a red skirt and white tank top, with sneakers on her feet and her brown hair tied back in a ponytail. Lord, she was the cutest goddamn thing he'd ever seen. And great, now he was thinking a woman was *cute*. Some manly man *he* was.

"You're avoiding me," she announced. When she noticed the grinning faces of Reed and AJ, she glanced over with a cheerful smile. "Hi, I'm Skyler. Nice to meet you." The smile vanished as she turned back to Gage. "Why are you avoiding me?"

Discomfort rolled around in his stomach. "I've been busy."

"Uh-huh. I'm sure you have." She narrowed her eyes. "My roommates told me not to bother coming here. They said I should just accept that you're not into me, and move on. Are they right?"

Reed spoke up before Gage could respond, sounding so

delighted by the situation that Gage wanted to slug him. "Oh, he's definitely into you, honey."

She looked intrigued. "Is he?"

"Trust me, he is. He's barely said one word to me about you."

"I didn't even know you existed," AJ piped up, green eyes twinkling.

Her frown swiftly returned. "You two aren't really painting a picture of a guy who's interested."

"With this idiot, that's exactly what it means." Reed jerked a thumb at Gage and rolled his eyes. "The less he says, the more interested he is."

Gage gritted his teeth. "Would you please stop talking about me like I'm not in the room?" He walked over and touched Skyler's arm. "Let's go talk somewhere private."

"Actually, leave the club altogether," Reed ordered. "Take a walk, see a movie, I don't care." His gaze shifted to Skyler. "Just get him out of here."

"It's Friday night," Gage said irritably. "I need to be on the floor."

"No, you need to be somewhere else. *Anywhere* else." Reed sounded just as annoyed. "You're strung too tight, bro. Snapping at customers, drinking—" He gestured to the beer bottle Gage had forgotten he was holding. "Take the night off, okay? We don't need a lawsuit on our heads after you snap and rough up the wrong person."

"We'll handle it," AJ said in a firm voice.

The deadly expressions on their faces told him not to argue. Crap. They were right, anyway. He *was* on edge. And it was only nine o'clock, way too early to already be feeling this way.

Skyler watched him expectantly, a flicker of concern in her eyes. "Gage?"

"Let's go," he muttered.

He released her arm, keeping a foot of distance between them as they made their way out of the club and emerged into the same alley where they'd first met.

"I'm sorry for barging in like that," she said sheepishly.

He nodded. "It's okay."

They wandered onto the main street, instantly dodging a group of rowdy young men barreling down the sidewalk. The city's downtown core was busy as hell on Friday nights, and Gage led Skyler to the edge of the sidewalk so they could avoid the rush of pedestrians. It was dark out, but the streetlamp behind them illuminated Skyler's face, bringing out the reddish highlights in her chestnut hair.

"I just had to know for sure," she added.

"Know what?" he said gruffly.

"If this is worth pursuing." Her hair fell over her shoulder as she slanted her head, and he resisted the urge to stroke the silky brown strands. "Is it?"

He gulped.

Tell her no.

What came out was, "Do you want to catch a movie or something?"

Chapter Seven

Skyler looked downright bewildered by the question, and Gage wasn't sure he blamed her. He was throwing off a serious case of mixed signals, yet for the life of him, he couldn't tell her to go. It had been easy to avoid her when all he had in front of him were words in a text message, but when she was standing right in front of him and looking so damn beautiful?

No amount of willpower in the world could force him to walk away.

After several seconds of silence, Skyler smirked at him. "Isn't that breaking the sex-only rule you enforced?"

"Yes or no," he said through clenched teeth.

She rolled her eyes. "You are the master of nonanswers, huh?" But she nodded anyway, her expression brightening. "You know what? Let's do it. I've been dying to see that new Stallone movie but nobody has wanted to go with me. My roommates hate action movies, so I always end up seeing them alone."

She liked action movies? Oh hell. She really was the woman of his dreams.

Skyler checked her phone, an adorable crease forming in her forehead as she scrolled through the listings. "Hey, it starts in thirty minutes. We can totally make it."

With that, she took off walking, leaving Gage no choice but to trail after her. He couldn't help but voice the question on his mind. "You don't mind going to the movies alone? A lot of people are way too embarrassed to do that."

Her dark ponytail bounced with each step. "Sometimes I prefer it, actually. And it doesn't embarrass me at all. I don't mind being alone."

"Me neither," he admitted.

"No, I think you prefer it, too." A thoughtful note crept in. "Were you a loner growing up?"

He shoved his hands in his pockets and shrugged. "Naah, I ran with a group of guys. We got into a shit-ton of trouble together."

"Did you grow up in Boston?"

"Southie, born and raised. You?"

"North End growing up, and then Beacon Hill when my mom remarried."

"Huh. I didn't take you for a rich girl."

"I'm not. My stepfather is."

They sidestepped a trio of giggling teenage girls and continued along at a brisk pace. Skyler didn't seem to mind walking, and he appreciated the hell out of that. Some women would balk at the thought of trekking eight blocks to see a movie, but Gage had a feeling nothing fazed Skyler. Ever.

"So you caused trouble as a kid," she mused. "And then you got older and chose to make a living by fighting."

He frowned. "You're doing a master's in psychology, huh? What, are you conducting a case study on me or something?"

"Nope. This is for my own private database. I'm trying to make sense of you."

"Don't bother. I'm not very complicated. What you see is

what you get."

"No, I don't think so at all." She came to a halt in the middle of the sidewalk and placed her hand on his chest. "Tell me the truth—do you like me?"

With those big eyes peering up at him and her soft hand resting between his pecs, he couldn't do anything but offer a wordless nod.

"Say it," she murmured.

"I—" His voice was so gravelly he had to clear his throat. "I like you."

Her lips curved in pleasure. "Then why were you avoiding me?"

"Because…" He swore softly. "I spent the night at your place."

"Yeah, and?"

"It's like you said before—I broke my own rule." Something akin to helplessness jammed in his chest. "Screwing is one thing. I know it. I'm good at it. But cuddling and whispering in bed? Whole other story."

He knew he sounded like an ass, but he'd set ground rules for a reason. He didn't want Skyler to get too attached. *He* didn't want to get too attached.

He'd hoped that enforcing a strict sex-only policy would help him keep a distance, but that night at Skyler's place… he'd forgotten all about it. Falling asleep tucked against her warm body had felt nice. Too damn nice.

"My friends told me today that there's no such thing as just sex." She pursed her lips. "I think they might be right. I mean, there's going to be moments when our man bits and lady bits aren't touching—"

He barked out a laugh.

"—which means we're bound to engage in some conversation. But that doesn't make things serious, though." Her hand remained on his chest, delicate fingers carelessly stroking him over his shirt.

Gage's hand traveled up and curled over hers, gently stroking her knuckles. "I don't do relationships, Skyler. I'm not good at them."

"Why do you think that?"

He swallowed. "Because I don't talk, I don't share my feelings, I'm not affectionate—I could probably list a dozen more things, but that's the gist of it."

"I see. Well. I hate to break it to you, big guy, but right now? You're talking, sharing your feelings, and being affectionate." She twisted her hand around and laced their fingers together as if to emphasize her point.

"That's not the same," he protested.

Skyler stuck out her tongue. "Stop being difficult." Her thumb rubbed the inside of his palm, and his cock instantly responded by jerking against his zipper. "Look, you like me, right?"

"I just said so, didn't I?" he rumbled.

"Do you like hanging out with me?"

He nodded warily.

She rose on her tiptoes, bringing those pouty lips close to his ear. "And you like being naked with me?"

A husky groan slipped out. "Damn it, baby, you know I do."

"Then let's keep doing it, all of it, and see where it goes. No promises, no pressure. If you don't feel like hanging out, just text me back and say, *not tonight*. I'm a big girl, Gage, and I won't cry myself to sleep if you don't feel like seeing me. Just don't ignore me altogether." She shot him a pointed stare. "Because that's a dick move."

He sheepishly avoided her eyes. "I know." He swallowed again, his voice coming out rusty. "I'm sorry."

"You're forgiven." She flashed a broad smile and tugged on his hand. "Okay, no more heavy, serious stuff. We'll be late for the movie if we don't hurry, and I don't want to miss a single second of Stallone."

· · ·

His hand was on her thigh. Good Lord. How was she supposed to concentrate on the screen when his *hand* was on her *thigh*? Not over her skirt, either. The insufferable man had pushed the fabric up so he could make contact with her bare skin.

Skyler couldn't believe they actually were sitting in a dark theater together. And Gage looked like he was actually enjoying himself, which was even more surprising. Movie dates hadn't been part of the deal, but no way was she complaining about this turn of events.

A sudden deafening explosion on the screen made her jump, summoning a dark chuckle from Gage. "Scaredy-cat," he whispered.

"I wasn't scared," she whispered back. "I was distracted."

He leaned into her, teasing her once more with his spicy, masculine scent. He smelled so darn good, and his sexy mouth was dangerously close to her ear. "What's got you so distracted, Skyler?"

She placed her hand over his and squeezed his knuckles. "*This*."

"Hmmm. Do you like it when I put my hands on you?" He spoke so softly she barely heard him over the gunfire and screeching tires blaring from the screen.

She stifled an aggravated sigh. "You know I do."

He moved his palm over her thigh in a sensual caress, chuckled again when her breath caught, and then stopped stroking and turned back to the action scene unfolding in front of them.

The theater was packed. Skyler was painfully aware of the people on either side of them, in front of them, behind them.

And she was equally aware of *him*. His long body folded into his chair, his biceps, sleek and tempting, peeking from the sleeves of his black T-shirt. If they'd been alone she would have spread her legs wider and given him access to more than her thigh, and Gage must have read her mind, because his mouth dipped close again.

"You're thinking about me fingering your pussy."

It took everything she had to stop a moan of lust from slipping out.

"I am, too," he rasped. "My cock is aching just picturing it."

Skyler's pulse drowned out the movie. Wonderful. Now she'd have to come back next week and watch it again, because Gage had officially stolen her ability to concentrate.

And he didn't let up—for the next hour, he whispered the dirtiest things in her ear. Seductive threats, wicked observations, filthy promises. His hand never left her thigh, but save for the occasional caress, it sat there in unmoving innocence as he taunted her with words and refused to follow through with actions. By the time the end credits rolled, she was squirming in her seat, panties soaked and nipples tight with arousal.

Skyler couldn't walk properly as they followed the mob out of the theater. She felt like she was running a fever, her body hot and achy and pleading for relief. Even though it was midnight, the air outside was so humid it only made her sweat harder. It was the hottest summer in Boston history, and she was with the hottest man in human history, a man who seemed determined to make her burst into flames.

"You okay, Sky?" he mocked. "It looks like you're having trouble walking."

She grabbed a hunk of his shirt and clenched her teeth as she glared at him. "You've been toying with me for the past hour and a half. Of course I'm not okay."

Gruff laughter rumbled out of his chest. He examined their surroundings for a beat, then took her hand and practically dragged her down the now-deserted street. Before she could blink, they were in another alley, with her back against a brick wall while a warm male hand traveled between her legs.

"What is it with you and alleys?" she mumbled.

He didn't answer. He just groaned, because his hand had discovered the evidence of her arousal in the form of her very drenched panties.

"Jesus. You *are* hurting." His gray eyes burned with passion. "My poor little bad girl."

God, he was teasing her again. Blunt fingertips lightly stroked her clit, his touch featherlight and not nearly enough. Skyler's head lolled to the side, but her eyes stayed open, fixed on the intensity sharpening his rugged features. Then something downright wicked flashed in his eyes and he slipped two fingers under the crotch of her panties.

After the endless torment of his verbal foreplay, her body was a lit fuse — and it exploded the second those long fingers drove deep. Skyler bit her lip as the orgasm shuddered through her. She bore down on Gage's fingers and rocked into his hand, but the rush of pleasure faded fast. It hadn't been enough, and he seemed to know it.

"That was just to take the edge off," he said huskily.

Skyler rearranged her skirt with trembling hands. "It didn't take the edge off at all," she grumbled. "I'm hurting even worse now."

"Aw, hell." He looked genuinely concerned for a moment, then brightened up. "Don't worry. I'll get you off again in the cab on the way home."

She choked back laughter as she followed him back to the street.

Chapter Eight

"Do you want to watch me fight tonight?"

That was the last thing Skyler expected to hear when she answered her phone. She didn't normally take calls at work, but when her cell had buzzed in her apron and she'd spotted Gage's number, she'd decided to make an exception. Although they'd seen and spoken to each other several times over the past week, it was still rare for him to be the one to reach out to her, so his taking the initiative to call brought a rush of happiness to her chest.

"I'm still working," she told him, genuine regret washing over her. Not that she was a big fan of watching grown men beat the crap out of each other, but she really did want to see Gage. She couldn't seem to get enough of the guy.

"What time are you done?" he asked.

"Well, we're closing early tonight for a private party. I'm not working it, but I am helping with the setup, so I won't be out of here until nine thirty-ish."

"Fight's not 'til ten." He paused. "Is that too late for you? I know you woke up early this morning, so if you want to go home and sleep, I understand."

His concern absolutely touched her. Honestly, she had no idea why he thought he sucked at relationships. He had an intense side, sure, but he also went out of his way to make sure her needs were met. Hell, he'd even cooked her dinner the other night. And he liked to *snuggle*. That already put him way ahead of her previous boyfriends.

"No, I want to see you fight," she told him. "I'll just chug some coffee at the end of my shift and I'll be wide-awake."

"You sure?"

"Positive."

"I'll pick you up at nine thirty then."

She was grinning like an idiot as she disconnected, same way she'd been grinning all week long. It was probably a good thing her roommates were always out, sparing her a ton of merciless teasing about how besotted she was.

She didn't understand it herself. Gage was the furthest thing from her type. Big, burly, and tattooed. Strong and silent. Lots of baggage. He avoided talking about his background, but she knew it haunted him, whatever it was. Still, the fact that he kept so much of himself hidden only made her want to work harder to unlock him.

Skyler ducked out of the employee lounge and spent the next hour tending to her customers and trading wisecracks with the chefs over the pickup counter. Since they were closing early, there weren't a lot of patrons left to serve—only two married couples, and a group of young men taking up residence in one of the rustic wooden booths against the back wall. The males flirted shamelessly with her as she dropped off their bill, but none of them sparked her interest. Nope, Gage was the only man capable of doing that.

She felt it the moment he walked into the steakhouse. Warmth flooded her body, the hairs on the back of her neck tingled, and sure enough, she turned to see him standing at the hostess stand, his hot gaze zeroing in on her like a missile. As her pulse sped up, Skyler smiled and gave a little wave, then gestured for him to wait at the bar.

He didn't smile back, just swept those gray eyes over her body, a slow and deliberate up-and-down that heated her cheeks. Her uniform was by no means indecent—black pants and a fitted blue dress shirt—but the way he looked at her, she might as well have been naked with a big bow tied around her.

Skyler swallowed, scowling when she glimpsed the amused gleam in his eyes. He knew how easily he got to her. Knew what he did to her with one sultry look.

As he wandered over to the bar, her gaze stayed glued on him. He wore a long-sleeve black shirt and faded blue jeans that hugged his taut ass. God, that ass. She knew firsthand how firm it was, how amazing it felt to dig her fingers into it while he moved on top of her.

"Holy moly, who is *that*?" One of the other waitresses sidled up to Skyler at the drink station, pretending to fan herself.

She couldn't wipe the enormous grin off her face. "My date."

Megan almost dropped dead from visible envy. "Goddamn it, girl, you did *good*."

"I know, right?"

It felt like forever before her shift ended. Once all the customers cleared out, the staff quickly began dragging tables to the center of the room to create one long eating area for the incoming party. As Skyler stacked chairs, she caught sight of her manager Naomi approaching Gage at the bar counter.

Naomi gestured to the door, clearly informing him he had to leave, which prompted Skyler to hurry over to the bar. "He's my ride home," she told her boss. "Is it cool if he hangs out here until I'm done?"

Naomi looked from Skyler to Gage, then back at Skyler, and gave an honest-to-God wink. "You know what, hon, why don't you take off now? We can handle the setup without you."

"Really?"

"Really. Go." With a barely restrained smirk, Naomi sauntered off.

"Jeez, I need you to pick me up more often," Skyler remarked. "Think of all the shifts I could have skipped out early on."

Gage slid off his stool and brushed a kiss on her lips, soft and fleeting and yet it still succeeded in curling her toes.

She fought to stop the goofy grin from resurfacing. "Can I wear this to the fight or should I go home and change first?"

He leaned in, his fingers toying with the strip of lace peeking out from her shirt. "What's this sexy lacy thing you've got on?"

God, his voice was like a drug. Deep and addictive.

"It's a camisole. But it's kind of skimpy—I usually wear something over it."

"Skimpy is fine. Trust me, the chicks at the arena will be wearing less clothing than that." He held out his hand, and she took it, shivering when their skin made contact.

Hand in hand, they left the restaurant and walked to the black Jeep Cherokee at the curb. Once she'd settled in the passenger seat, Skyler unbuttoned her shirt, noting with a grin that Gage's gaze followed every minute motion of her fingers. When the shirt parted and she slid it off her shoulders, he released a growling sound that heated the car.

"Damn, that *is* skimpy. I love it."

Pleasure danced inside her. His appreciative gaze did wonders for her ego. She was fully aware that she wasn't supermodel-gorgeous, but gosh darn it, Gage made her feel like she was.

His hand rested on her thigh during the entire drive across town. What he'd referred to as the arena ended up being an enormous warehouse in the city's west end. Gage pulled into the jam-packed parking lot in front of the sprawling gray building and drove up to a row of reserved spaces. After he'd killed the engine, he hopped out and rounded the vehicle to open Skyler's door.

And her friends said chivalry was dead.

Two minutes later they strode into the building, and Skyler was astonished by the number of people crammed inside of it. Bleachers spanned three of the arena's walls, while the fourth housed a bar area with a mile-long line.

The crowd was surprisingly eclectic. The Irish folks were easy to spot thanks to their thick brogues and the pints of Guinness in their hands. The hipsters looked bored by it all—they were probably there ironically, anyway—and Skyler also glimpsed several groups of businessmen in the bleachers. Some people were covered in tattoos, some weren't. Some women wore sneakers, others wore heels. And almost everyone was screaming their lungs out, all eyes focused on the cage in the center of the room. It boasted ominous chain-link walls, and a large fighting surface covered with faint reddish stains. Blood, Skyler realized. Wiped away, but not entirely.

Two men were locked together in the corner of the cage, one curled over on the mat and locked into submission by the one above him. Even from where she stood, Skyler saw the veins bulging in the captive man's forehead. He was red-faced and gasping, meaty fists pounding upward at the man trapping him in the hold. But to no avail. Several seconds passed before the man's shoulders slumped and he slowly tapped the mat.

As the crowd roared, the winner hopped up and raised his arms in a victory pose.

"I asked for an early slot, so I should probably head over

to the locker room now." Gage led her to the bleachers and found an empty seat, then gestured for her to sit. "You'll be okay here, but if anyone gives you trouble, tell them you're with me."

She nodded. "So what do I say to you? Break a leg? Kick his ass?"

"Good luck will do just fine."

"Good luck then." She stood on her tiptoes and smacked a kiss on his cheek.

He smiled, and a second later he was swallowed up by the crowd.

Skyler turned her attention to the cage, where the next fight was starting. This one featured an African-American man with full-sleeve tattoos and a beefy opponent with a shaved head that gleamed beneath the bright lights. While the previous match had resembled wrestling, this one looked more like boxing.

Skyler watched with wide eyes as the fists began to fly. She couldn't hear anything but the roar of the fans, but she imagined the sounds of flesh slapping flesh, hard thumps and sickening crunches. Two women next to her screeched like banshees, cheering for the dark-skinned man, while a group of guys in the row behind her boomed out encouragements for the stocky fellow.

Lord. She was definitely leaving here tonight with a migraine.

By the time the buzzer sounded and the final round ended, Skyler was wondering what all the appeal was—and then she spotted Gage, and the answer became pretty darn clear.

He was barefoot and bare-chested, black shorts hanging off his trim hips and skin already glistening from the hot, stifling air. His sculpted muscles were sheer perfection, and his tattoos stood out against his tanned flesh. He looked like a warrior. A deadly, sexy warrior, and her body instantly reacted to the waves of raw masculinity rolling off him.

The announcer stepped up to introduce the two fighters, and a spark of displeasure ignited in Skyler's belly when she registered the obscene amount of female screams triggered by Gage's introduction. Clearly her man had a fan club.

Gage's opponent was bulkier but several inches shorter, with a scary-looking skull tattoo that spanned his entire chest. Definitely someone she would run in the other direction from if she saw him on the street, and yet the second the thought struck, she scolded herself for being so judgmental. For all she knew, Skull Tattoo was a really sweet guy. A guy who liked to stay home and watch *Everybody Loves Raymond* reruns with his wife and only fought on the weekends to make money for their couples' pottery classes.

Except then he bellowed out an animal roar and dragged his finger across his throat in a death promise to Gage, and Skyler promptly went back to disliking him.

Gage, however, was completely unruffled. Even from yards away, Skyler noticed nothing but pure calm reflecting in his eyes.

She jerked when a bell rang to indicate the start of the first round. Her heart immediately jumped to her throat when Skull Tattoo launched himself at Gage. Fists up, Gage blocked his opponent's blows, then attacked so fast Skyler barely even saw him move.

Left hook, right hook, one-two punches at lightning speed, until he'd backed Skull Tattoo against the chain-link wall. All the other man could do was try to defend himself, but when he threw his hands up to protect his face, Gage simply planted a fist in the man's gut. Skull Tattoo buckled over, swayed on his feet, and then lifted his head in time for Gage's fist to connect with the side of his face.

Lights out.

It was over.

Skyler stood there, dumbfounded. Her jaw dropped as two refs and a man who must have been the doctor rushed over to the unconscious fighter. The doctor touched his cheek, checked his pupils, and then signaled something to the ref, who wasted no time thrusting Gage's arm up in the air. The announcer declared Gage the winner and the crowd went wild.

Unlike the previous victor, Gage didn't stick around to take a bow or pump his fists. Covered in sweat, he hopped out of the cage and made a beeline for the row of chairs in front of it. Skyler saw him mutter something to a man with ginger hair and a bushy beard. People's heads blocked their faces from view, but she noted Gage's stiff body language, and knew he wasn't happy with the conversation.

A moment later, he stalked back to the locker rooms.

Since she didn't care about the next fight, Skyler left her seat and headed in the direction Gage had gone, but the two beefy men guarding the corridor wouldn't let her through. She swallowed her irritation and stepped back to wait.

Fortunately, Gage reappeared less than five minutes later, back in his street clothes and showing no signs of injury. Not even a bruise.

Then again, no duh. His opponent hadn't gotten a single swing in.

"Hey." His face softened when he saw her.

"Hey. Nice match." She raised one eyebrow. "Are all your fights usually so quick?"

"Nope." He brought his head close to hers and lowered his voice. "I wanted it over fast so I could take you home and fuck you."

"You say the sweetest things." Her heart soared when he flashed her a crooked grin. She loved seeing his lips curve like that. It was so rare, and so deliciously rewarding when it happened. "So is that it, or are we sticking around to watch the other fights?"

"Do you want to?"

She winced when another roar went through the crowd. "God, no. My head is going to explode from all this screaming."

They were out of the arena less than thirty minutes after they'd gotten there, Gage's phone ringing just as they reached his car. He pulled it out, frowned at the number, then muttered, "Give me a sec," before taking several steps away.

It couldn't be considered eavesdropping when the other person wasn't bothering to lower their voice, right?

Because there was no way *not* to hear Gage's ferocious, "Are you kidding me?"

Skyler flinched at the note of fury in his tone, wondering who the caller was. She'd never seen Gage this upset before.

"Just stay there. I'm on my way over." Anger lined his strides as he walked back to the car. "Change of plans," he said roughly. "I'm taking you home, but I can't stay over tonight."

"What's wrong?"

"I need to go see my brother."

"I'll come with you," she said instantly.

Gage hesitated, looking so unhappy with the idea she felt a tad insulted.

"Are you expecting any trouble?" she asked pointedly.

"No, probably not. I doubt it'll even take too long, but—"

"Then it makes even more sense for me to come along," she interrupted. "We can stop in on your brother, and then head to my place like we originally intended."

"Sky..." His tone was laced with reluctance.

"If you're worried about this being some kind of big relationship step, then don't. It's just your brother—it's not like I'm meeting your parents or anything. What's the harm in letting me tag along?" She knew she was pushing him, but she couldn't seem to stop. She wanted another glimpse, just one more tiny glimpse into Gage's life. She'd gotten one now at the arena, but it wasn't enough. She wanted more, darn it.

"Please?" she said softly.

After a long pause, he let out a weary curse. "Fine, you can come. We won't be there long, anyway." Then he sighed. "C'mon, let's go."

Chapter Nine

Gage's brother lived in a converted town house that consisted of four apartments. Denny's was on the ground floor with an entrance located at the side of the brick house, and the lightbulb over the door shone bright when Gage and Skyler walked up.

Gage reached for the screen door, glancing at the woman by his side. "You can wait out here if you want."

He found himself praying she'd agree. Denny had sounded alert and sober on the phone, but you never knew with him. Gage had once seen his brother carry on an entire conversation with two police officers while tripping on half a dozen hits of acid.

Crap, why had he let Skyler convince him to bring her?

Because you can't say no to the damn woman.

Nope, he certainly couldn't. All it had taken was the disappointed glimmer in her beautiful eyes and her soft "please" and he'd caved like a cheap tent.

Except…it was more than that. A part of him had wanted her to come. Maybe if she met Denny, if she saw what Gage had to deal with, she'd…what? Understand him better? Understand why he couldn't give her more than a fling?

"I'll come in with you," she said, her quiet voice interrupting his troubled thoughts.

His head jerked in a nod. He was about to stick his key in the lock when the door swung open and his brother appeared.

Gage instantly ran through the usual routine—examined Denny's pupils, checked his bare arms for fresh track marks, inhaled deeply for any lingering scents of crack or heroin. But Denny looked as sober as he'd sounded earlier, and the only odor hanging in the air was the faint whiff of pot smoke.

"Hey," Denny said awkwardly.

"Hey." Gage cleared his throat. "This is Skyler."

"Nice to meet you." His brother stuck out his hand, which Skyler tentatively shook. "Come in. I don't want to talk out here."

They followed him inside, where the smell of marijuana got stronger. "You're smoking weed again?" Gage couldn't hide his disapproval.

Denny was ahead of them so his face was hidden from view, but his shoulders sagged at the accusation. "No, Gage, I'm not smoking weed again. I'm also not drinking, mainlining H, popping E and acid, or smoking crack. I'm clean, just like I've been for the last three months."

No bitterness in his voice, just tired resignation. He led them to the living room, where Gage noticed all the windows had been cranked open to let in fresh air. His brother went to sit on the couch, but Gage remained standing. Skyler ended up in the plaid upholstered recliner, timidly crossing her legs together.

Nobody spoke for several long moments. As Gage stared at his kid brother, an eddy of familiar emotions churned in his gut. Disappointment, sorrow, pain, disgust. Despite the seven-year age difference between the brothers, their resemblance was uncanny, especially now that Denny had stopped poisoning his body and was no longer gaunt and sickly looking. They both had the same gray eyes and dark hair, just like their old man.

Only while Gage was nothing like their father, Denny had certainly followed in Bobby Holt's self-destructive footsteps. Smoking weed by the time he was thirteen, addicted to crack by seventeen, graduating to heroin at twenty. And everything got substantially worse when Denny went to work for O'Donnell's crew. Addicts had no business selling drugs, and Mitch O'Donnell had pounced on the opportunity to capitalize on Denny's weakness.

"I won't bother with small talk or pretend you're here to shoot the shit with your kid brother," Denny said. "Mitch sent some of his thugs over about an hour ago."

Gage's stomach went rigid. "Yeah? What'd they want?"

"According to them? Just to say hi." Denny didn't sound convinced, and neither was Gage. "It was Paddy and Roy— you remember them, right? They showed up at my door, acting like we were long-lost bros."

"You let them in?"

Denny gave an uneasy nod. "Didn't have much of a choice. They pretty much walked inside like they'd been invited. But they didn't stay long. Lit up a couple of joints, cracked some jokes, filled me in on what's been happening with the old crew." He paused. "Roy had heroin on him. They tried to get me to use."

Hot fury boiled in Gage's gut. Fucking sons of bitches.

"And before you assume the worst, I said no. They kept poking and prodding, using that peer pressure bullshit, bringing up old times. I stood my ground, told them I was sober now, and they left."

Other people might have felt a burst of pride that Denny had resisted temptation, but not Gage. It was too late for *pride*. Denny could be clean for the next fifty years of his life, and it still wouldn't erase all the shit he'd put Gage through.

"I think they were trying to knock me off the wagon." Denny sounded sad, broken even.

"Why would anyone do that?" Skyler blurted out. "Deliberately try to tempt an addict—you are an addict, right?" When Denny nodded, her eyes flashed with anger. "That's just cruel."

"That's Mitch for you," Gage's brother muttered.

"Who's Mitch?" Her tentative question lingered in the air, spurring Denny to glance at Gage in surprise.

"She doesn't know?"

He shrugged.

"Any of it?" Denny prompted.

"We only recently met," Gage said gruffly. "I hadn't gotten around to it."

He felt her watching him but couldn't bring himself to look at her. His jaw had clenched so tight his molars ached. Fuck. Bringing Skyler had been a mistake. He should have followed his instincts and stuck to his guns, damn it. He didn't want her here. He didn't want her involved.

Unfortunately, his brother took it upon himself to involve her. "Mitch O'Donnell runs the drug game in Southie," Denny said grimly. "I used to deal for him."

"Oh."

Gage swallowed his rage. He hated that Skyler had to hear any of this. Hell, he could practically see his darkness oozing toward her like a puddle of black tar. He should've known better than to show her this part of his life.

"He's also a fight promoter and part owner of the arena where Gage fights," Denny added.

Skyler wrinkled her brow as she turned to Gage. "You fight for a drug dealer?"

He sighed. "O'Donnell is a respectable business owner

on paper. And I don't fight for him. I'm just repaying a debt."

"My debt," Denny supplied in a sour voice. "I messed up, and now Gage is paying the price."

Skyler's confusion seemed to heighten. "What did you do?"

Gage took an abrupt step toward the doorway. "We should go. Denny, thanks for giving me the heads-up about — "

"I stole from Mitch," Denny cut in, focused wholly on Skyler. "I was a pathetic junkie and I smoked a shipment instead of selling it. And when you steal from O'Donnell, you don't get a slap on the wrist. You get cement shoes at the bottom of the harbor."

She looked alarmed. "He threatened you?"

"Of course." Denny's voice cracked. "But Gage struck a deal for me."

He felt those big blue eyes on his face again. "He's *making* you fight?" Skyler said in horror.

Frustration climbed up his chest and curled around his throat like a cold fist. "It's not a big deal, Sky." Christ, he needed to get out of here.

"Gage, it *is* a big deal."

"I've got one fight left and then I'm done." He spared a glance at his brother. "And then *we're* done."

"I know."

Denny's expression was so tormented he had to look away. Lord, he couldn't breathe all of a sudden. And his hands felt like icy blocks.

"I'll handle Mitch, okay?" Gage muttered. "But you realize what he's trying to do, right?"

"He wants you to keep fighting for him," Denny said flatly.

"Not gonna happen. But as a precaution I think you should leave town for a couple weeks. Normally I'd suggest laying low here in the city, but Mitch will just send someone to find you again. He'll try to use you against me."

"Don't worry, I'm actually leaving for Maine the day after tomorrow. My girlfriend's family has a house on the coast. We're spending the month there."

"Girlfriend?" It was almost depressing how little knowledge he had about his own brother's life.

"Yeah. Maggie." Denny's eyes softened. "We met after I got out of rehab. She's a middle-school teacher."

Gage just nodded.

"I'll leave you a number where you can reach me. I don't have my old cell anymore, and I haven't gotten a new one yet."

With another curt nod, Gage headed for the door. It took a second to realize Skyler hadn't followed, and he turned to find her giving Denny a quick hug. "Be careful," he heard her murmur. "And stay strong, okay?"

Even though it grated to see her reassure a man who didn't deserve it, Gage couldn't fault her for it. The woman was a goddamn saint. He'd known it from the moment he met her.

"Gage."

His brother's voice stopped him at the door. "What?" he mumbled, turning to face Denny.

"I really am sorry. And I meant what I said three months ago. I *will* make this up to you." An awkward pause followed. "I'll prove to you that you can trust me."

After a beat, he stiffly turned away from Denny's sad gray eyes. "I'll believe it when I see it."

• • •

"I still feel like we should have stayed. What if those guys come back?" Biting her bottom lip, Skyler glanced at Gage in concern, but his hard gaze remained focused on the road ahead.

"They won't. Mitch was just testing the waters, trying to get a sense of Denny's state of mind. He probably thought he could use Denny again to extend our arrangement, but now that he knows Denny can't be pushed off the wagon, he'll back off."

Despite the reassurance, Skyler's mild concern mutated into bone-deep worry. God, she hated, *hated* the thought of Gage putting his own life on the line for a mistake he hadn't even made.

"How many fights did you commit to?" she asked.

"Ten."

The response sent a jolt of anger spiraling through her, the volatile emotion directed solely at Gage's brother. Yes, Denny had looked and sounded repentant, but as the weight of his actions suddenly sank in, Skyler couldn't muster up any more sympathy. "Your brother should have taken responsibility for his own mistake."

"It's not that simple."

She knew she sounded callous, but the realization that Gage was in physical danger because of his brother was too damn maddening. Besides, she'd always been a big believer in facing the consequences of your own actions.

"If a drug dealer wants to hurt him, then that's *his* problem. Maybe he shouldn't have gotten involved with the drug dealer to begin with."

"Not hurt," Gage corrected, "*Kill*. O'Donnell and his crew don't mess around, Skyler. They would've slit Denny's throat and dumped his body in the river, make no mistake about it. He didn't have the cash to pay them back, and he couldn't have worked off the debt—a junkie drug dealer can't be trusted. If Denny had been anyone else, Mitch would've killed him in a heartbeat, but Denny happens to be my brother, and Mitch has been dying to have some leverage over me."

"So he spared your brother's life just to get you to fight?"

"Pretty much. There's a lot of money in MMA tournaments these days, especially if you're good. And I'm good."

She didn't doubt it. Heck, she'd seen him knock a man unconscious with one punch tonight.

"Mitch and I grew up together, and he was pissed when I didn't want to go into the drug business with him. He approached me when I first started fighting—he wanted to be my manager and hook me up with his trainer. When I turned him down, he didn't like it one damn bit. So after Denny screwed up, Mitch had me right where he wanted me."

It occurred to her that this was the most Gage had said to her at one time. No bare-minimum responses tonight, no attempt to hide the pain in his eyes. Seeing his brother had obviously upset him more than he'd let on.

"You've cleaned up a lot of Denny's messes, haven't you?" she said quietly.

His defeated nod brought an ache to her heart. "I'm just a regular old janitor. I can't even remember how many times I've had to drag him out of the gutter. Dozens of ER visits, four ODs. I've cleaned up his vomit, wiped up his blood, stitched up his wounds." Gage shook his head in visible disgust. "I tried to talk him out of going to work for Mitch, but Denny is a stubborn asshole and wouldn't listen. But I'm done now. I promised myself that after I paid off his debt, I would never bail him out again. He's on his own now."

Skyler reached across the center console and touched his hand over the gearshift. She was beginning to understand where all his guarded intensity stemmed from, why he kept his emotions under lock and key and refused to speak about his past. Clearly he'd lived a hard life, sacrificing much of it for his younger brother.

"I'm sorry you had to see that." His abrupt apology startled her, and when he gave her a sideways glance, the shamed expression on his face stunned her even more. "I know I was harsh on him, but there's no goodwill left in me anymore. I must have come off as an asshole, though, and I'm sorry."

"You have nothing to be sorry for. We all have our family stuff."

He made a cynical noise. "I'm not sure I believe you have any 'family stuff.'"

"Probably not as bad as yours, but I didn't have the greatest time growing up, either," she admitted. "My parents fought all the time, and I was constantly caught in the middle. My dad wanted them to go to couples counseling, but Mom refused, and eventually she cheated on him with another man. I lived with her and my stepdad after the divorce."

"Did you still see your dad often?"

"He died of a heart attack a year after she left him." Skyler fought a rush of sadness. "Mom died, too, about five years ago. Car accident."

He lightly stroked her knuckles. "I'm sorry." He hesitated. "Is that why you want to be a therapist? Do you think your parents would have stayed together if they saw one?"

"I don't know. Maybe. I have considered treating couples once I get my license, but I haven't decided yet."

"I think you'll make a great therapist," he said gruffly.

"I hope so."

He stopped at a red light, then glanced over again. "My place is up the street. Do you want to go there, or should I take you home?"

"No, let's stay at your place." She lived at least another fifteen minutes away, which seemed way too long to wait. Right now, she wanted nothing more than to slide into bed with Gage and spend the night in his arms.

He turned onto a pretty residential street and parked at the curb. His town house was tall and skinny like his brother's, but it wasn't split into apartments. He had three stories all to himself, but as she discovered a few minutes later, he didn't seem at all interested in decorating. The house boasted bare walls, very little furniture, and no personal touches, reminding Skyler of her own minimalist style.

"Do you want something to drink?" He flicked on a light in the front hall. "Coffee, tea? Or maybe something stronger?"

"I'll have whatever you're having."

She followed him down a narrow corridor to the kitchen, which was cozier than she expected. It had cherry-stained cupboards, black granite counters, and a large wooden table surrounded by four tall-backed chairs. She smiled when she noticed the rows of cookbooks on a shelf over the stove, and the dozen colorful mugs hanging from hooks next to the sink.

"I think I need the strong stuff." Gage opened a cupboard and grabbed a bottle of Jack Daniel's. "You sure you want some?"

"Yeah. I could use a drink."

She accepted the shot glass he handed her and tapped it against his, then took a quick swig of whiskey. A small amount, but it still burned her throat and tingled in her belly. She'd been on edge ever since they'd gone to Denny's house, but the alcohol relaxed her almost immediately.

Gage, however, didn't look the slightest bit relaxed, not even after he drank a second shot. His shoulders were set in a rigid line as he dropped their glasses in the sink.

After a beat of hesitation, Skyler wrapped her arms around him from behind and rested her head between his shoulder blades. As expected, he instantly tried to sidestep, but she held on tighter. "Would you just let me hug you? You had a crappy night, big guy. You need a hug."

He sagged into the physical contact. "I'm fine."

"No, you're not. You're in pain." She planted a kiss on the center of his back. Her lips touched the fabric of his shirt and not bare skin, but the soft peck still had an effect on him because he shuddered slightly. "I'm sorry about your brother, Gage. I'm sorry you keep having to sacrifice yourself for him."

With a ragged breath, he turned around and kissed her. She tasted the alcohol on his lips, the desperation on his tongue. When he fisted her hair to pull her closer, she welcomed the delicious sting on her scalp. She loved his rough grip, the husky sounds he made whenever their tongues touched.

When he tried to deepen the kiss, she smiled and moved her lips away, gliding them along his strong jawline. She peppered kisses down to his neck, then licked his warm skin and experienced a rush of dizziness as his masculine taste infused her senses.

"Let's go upstairs," he murmured. "I need to make it up to you. I didn't like getting so angry in front of you."

"No, this isn't about me." Her hands slipped to his waist, undoing his jeans so she could reach inside his boxer-briefs. "This is about making *you* feel better. I know seeing him tonight was hard on you."

"Skyler…" His head lolled to the side when her fingers closed around his cock.

"Let me take care of you," she whispered, and then she sank to her knees in front of him and gently freed his erection from his pants.

"You don't have to take care of me."

His awkward protest didn't surprise her. She got the feeling he didn't let *anyone* take care of him. Oh no, he kept his emotions bottled up, forever holding a part of himself back.

"I *want* to," she said firmly.

Her tongue moved in a delicate lick around his crown, drawing a hoarse groan from him. She wanted to go slow, to tease and prolong his pleasure, but she knew that wasn't what he needed right now. His hips were already pushing forward, his cock seeking the warmth of her mouth, so she gave it to him. She swallowed his thick shaft, sucking hard and fast, each urgent stroke intensifying her own desire.

Gage came a moment later with an anguished moan, cupping the back of her head as the hot jets of his release filled her mouth. She sucked him dry, then planted soft licks and kisses on his still-hard shaft, waiting for him to come down, for his breathing to steady. When she lifted her head, the haze of pleasure and adoration swimming in his eyes stole her breath.

He hauled her to her feet, kissed her so hard she gasped, then broke them apart so he could meet her eyes. "Thank you for coming with me to Denny's tonight." A faint grin sprang to his lips. "And thank you for making me come."

She grinned back. "You're welcome. Now let's go and find a bed so I can take care of you some more."

Chapter Ten

Gage experienced a sense of déjà vu as he fixed his gaze on the back booth and found Skyler's blue eyes twinkling at him. She wasn't sitting next to another man this time, but just like the night they'd met, she still only had eyes for him.

And he only had eyes for *her.* There'd been a subtle shift deep inside him these past two weeks. Ever since he'd taken her to his brother's place, he'd been startled to notice that he was no longer pushing her away, but pulling her closer. Every time he saw her, another layer of his inner shield seemed to crumble, which probably would've worried him if he weren't so damn infatuated with the woman.

And apparently he wasn't the only one to notice the change in him.

"Aw, hell, you're a total goner." Reed came up beside him, sounding resigned as he followed Gage's gaze. "So it's official? My little boy has himself a girlfriend?"

He shrugged. "Nah, it's still casual, just like it's always been."

"Bullshit. You're making googly eyes at her, for chrissake.

There is *nothing* casual about googly eyes." Reed waggled his brows. "When can I expect my wedding invitation?"

Gage scowled at his friend. "Stop being a brat." Then he caught Skyler's gaze again, and the smile she flashed him damn near melted his heart.

Crap. Maybe Reed was right. When one pretty smile succeeded in getting a man all warm and weak-kneed, didn't that in fact make him a goner?

He turned back to Reed. "I'm going over to say hi. Coming?"

Although technically he was still working, there was nothing wrong with making a quick stop at the booth to say hello to Skyler and AJ's girlfriend, Darcy, who'd accompanied Skyler to the club tonight. The two women had hit it off last week when the group had gone for beer and wings at a pub near AJ's place, and their insta-connection hadn't surprised Gage one bit. Darcy was the most outgoing person he'd ever met, with the kind of bubbly, magnetic personality that made everyone around her feel at ease.

Well, maybe not *everyone*—Reed was the only one who seemed immune to her charm. He was always civil to her, but Gage hadn't missed the way his friend tensed up whenever AJ's girl was around.

That tension was present now, prompting him to lower his voice and say, "Seriously, man, what's your problem with Darcy?"

"Nothing." Reed shrugged. "We don't have much in common, that's all."

"You don't need to have anything in common with her— you're not dating her, AJ is. And he's happy as fuck with her, so the least you could do is be nice." Gage shook his head in disapproval. "Whatever. I'm going to say hi. Stay here if you want."

He kept a vigilant eye on the other patrons as he crossed

the lounge, but everything seemed fine, security-wise. Reed ended up coming with him, reluctance lining his long strides all the way to the ladies' booth.

"Hi." Gage couldn't keep the goofy grin off his face as he greeted Skyler.

"Hi." She responded with another smile, this one loaded with heat as she swept her gaze up and down his body.

She'd told him more than once how much she loved him in a wifebeater. Supposedly he had "wicked hot arms" and the way she was blatantly admiring them now triggered a hefty dose of lust. Lord, he couldn't wait to get her naked later.

He just hoped he wouldn't be too banged up from the fight. Though he was perfectly happy to deal with a few more cuts and bruises, seeing as how this would be the last time.

Tonight was his last fight.

Last. Fucking. Fight.

Once he walked out of that cage, he'd never have to go back in. Denny's debt would be paid, and Gage would finally be free of Mitch O'Donnell for good.

"Gage," Darcy said cheerfully, her blue eyes sparkling with mischief. "Sky and I were just talking about you."

He slanted his head. "Yeah?"

"Oh yeah. Well, actually, we were talking about those ridiculously sexy arms of yours." Darcy tucked a strand of strawberry-blond hair behind her ear, then fanned herself with one hand like a Southern belle. "You're looking damn good, babe. I think I might have to persuade AJ to ink himself up. I never realized how hot tattoos were." As her gaze shifted to Reed, her tone grew wary. "Hey, Reed."

"Darcy." He shoved his hands in the back pockets of his black jeans. "You ladies having fun?"

She gestured to the four empty shot glasses on the tabletop. "Hell yeah we are." She grinned. "On a related note, I think you boys will need to call us a cab later. Sky and I will be way too plastered to drive."

Reed frowned. "Are you sure getting loaded is a good idea?"

Darcy threw her head back and laughed. "It's girls' night. Getting loaded is the one and only requirement."

Skyler nodded in agreement. "Definitely." She winked at Gage. "You don't mind, right?"

He nearly swallowed his tongue at the coy question. He'd seen Skyler drunk only once: last weekend when they'd split a twelve-pack during an action movie marathon. And he could honestly say he'd never had more fun watching a woman get sloshed. With her cheeks flushed and her eyes shining, she'd chattered a mile a minute throughout every movie—and proceeded to end the night performing an hour-long striptease for him, followed by a blow job for the ages.

Greatest night of his life.

"I don't mind at all," he drawled.

Skyler hesitated. "You sure? Because I'm happy to come to the arena with you."

She'd already offered several times, and he gave her the same answer as before—a quick shake of his head.

"Are you sure?" she pressed.

"Positive. I really don't want to make a big thing out of it," he admitted. "I just want to finish the match and leave. I'll meet you at your place when it's done, okay?"

"Sounds good."

"Sounds *great*," Darcy corrected. "That gives us lots and lots of time for dirty girl talk and shooters."

Next to Gage, Reed had begun edging away. "I'll leave you to it then. Find me when you're ready to go and I'll arrange for a taxi."

Darcy blew him a kiss. "You're a prince, Reedford."

"You know my full name isn't Reedford, right?"

"But it sounds so much more distinguished," she

protested.

Reed looked like he was fighting a laugh, but then his eyes went shuttered and he glanced at Gage. "I'm heading upstairs to look over those liquor orders. Later, bro."

The moment Reed was gone, a male voice boomed out of Gage's earpiece. "We've got trouble at the front door, boss," one of the bouncers reported. "Three douche bags refusing to wait in line. They're trying to rough Leo up."

"On my way," he said briskly. He clicked the earpiece and looked at Skyler. "Duty calls. See you later?"

"Yep."

He leaned in to plant a brief kiss on her lips, then stalked off to take care of business.

. . .

Two hours later, Gage was taping up his hands just as Mitch strode into the locker room.

"What's up?" he muttered without a shred of enthusiasm. He'd been expecting the visit, but that didn't mean he was looking forward to it.

Mitch cocked his head at the two other men loitering near the locker banks. "Can we have a minute, boys?"

The fighters nodded, leaving the room without delay. Once they were alone, Mitch fixed his shrewd dark eyes on Gage. "So."

He raised a brow. "So."

"After tonight you've filled your end of our arrangement."

"Well aware of that." Rising from the bench, Gage tucked his shirt, pants, and boots into an empty locker behind him.

"I have a proposition for you." Mitch leaned against the cinder-block wall, his expression thoughtful.

Gage slammed the locker door and turned to face the other man. "Not interested."

"You haven't even heard me out yet." Irritation flashed in Mitch's eyes. "At least show me the fucking courtesy of listening."

Stifling a curse, he folded his arms over his chest. "All right. Let's hear it."

"There's a tournament in eight weeks."

Gage stayed quiet.

"It's an elimination tourney. Prize is half a million bucks…"

He still didn't answer.

"I want to sponsor you."

His silence continued.

"Nicky over at Sal's gym is willing to train you. I'll put up the entry fee, and if you win or place, we split the cash fifty-fifty. Whadda you say?"

Gage looked Mitch in the eye and said, "No."

The other man swore in annoyance. "Fine, I'm willing to go sixty-forty, but that's it."

"I don't care about the cash. I'm not entering." He flopped down on the bench again and planted both hands on his thighs, the look on his face brooking no argument.

"Come on, man, just think about it. It'll only cost you two days of your time, and if you win you'll earn a cool two hundred and fifty G's. If you place you'll get a hundred. Easy money, brother."

"I already have a day job," Gage said curtly. "I'm part owner of a very successful club. That's where I want to be."

"I'm sure your partners will give you time off if you—"

"You're not hearing me. I *want* to be there. I have no interest in fighting anymore, which is what I told you three months ago. I only agreed to these matches because you backed me into a corner, but we're square now." Gage shot the other man a dark look. "You're a man of your word, or at least that's what you like to tell everyone. Isn't that right?"

Mitch's jaw tensed. "My word is gold, Gage."

"Then prove it. I've carried out my end of the deal, now it's your turn. After tonight, you leave me and Denny alone."

A long silence fell over them. Anger, frustration, and resentment twisted O'Donnell's face into an expression so volatile Gage almost expected to have to fight the guy. But after several more seconds ticked by, the other man backed off. "Fine. Your loss. If you want to throw away this opportunity, then go for it. But FYI—it makes you a fucking idiot."

"Then I'm a fucking idiot." Gage flashed a humorless smile. "Will you tell LeSean to grab me when it's time for my match?"

Mitch scowled. Nodded. Then stalked out of the room.

In a flash, a colossal weight was lifted off Gage's chest.

When LeSean came to get him thirty minutes later, Gage walked out of the locker room with an actual spring in his step. Genuinely looking forward to climbing in the cage tonight, knowing it was the last time he'd ever have to do it. And once that final bell rang, he'd get the hell outta there and head to Skyler's house, where he'd spend the whole night in her arms.

Life was finally looking up again.

Chapter Eleven

"Remind me to get you in a good mood more often." Skyler gasped as Gage rolled off her and collapsed on his back.

"Baby, I'm always in a good mood when I'm with you."

The smile he flashed made her heart pound. He'd been doing that a lot this week. Smiling. Laughing. Saying the sweetest darn things. He was a gazillion times more relaxed since his last fight, and she was reaping the rewards of it.

"Do you want to watch a movie or something?" She shifted onto her side and propped up on one elbow. "Oooh, or maybe we can go downstairs, and you can show me how to prepare that yummy stir-fry you made the other night—" Her phone buzzed on the nightstand. "Hold that thought." She leaned over to check the screen, frowned, then kept talking. "Anyway, should we—"

"Don't *anyway* me," he chided. "Who just texted?"

A sigh lodged in her throat. "My stepfather."

"What did he want?"

"Nothing, really. He calls or texts every few weeks to say hi. Asks if I want to have lunch or dinner or whatever."

Gage studied her face, his dark brows drawn together. "Why do you look so upset, then? You don't like him?"

"No, it's not that…" Hesitation tightened her chest. "It's just…no matter how hard I try, I can't stop viewing him as the man who broke up my parents' marriage. And yeah, I know it takes two to cheat. It wasn't entirely Clay's fault—Mom was at fault, too. But every time I see him, I think of my dad, and how brokenhearted he was when Mom left, and…" Her throat closed up. "I know I'm not being fair to Clay, but I can't help the way I feel."

"Did he ever remarry?"

"No. And he doesn't have any other kids." She bit the inside of her cheek. "Do you think I'm awful for ignoring him?"

"Not at all. I think you've gotta do what's right for you."

She fell quiet for a moment, resting her head against his chest and listening to the steady beating of his heart. "What about your parents? What are they like?"

"Oh, it's the usual sob story." He spoke in a monotone voice. "My dad was a deadbeat. Raging alcoholic, petty criminal. He got arrested for armed robbery about ten years ago. Still in prison as far as I know."

"And your mom?"

Now that deep voice thickened with pain. "She was a good woman. Gentle, compassionate. She died of cancer when I was eleven." He lightly tapped the tattoo on his chest. "I put her initials here when I turned sixteen. I guess I wanted a reminder that there really are some good people in this world."

"I wondered what those stood for." Skyler traced each letter carefully, experiencing a wave of sadness. "I'm sorry about your mom."

"I'm sorry about yours."

A comfortable silence settled over them. It was the

one thing she'd never expected—the comfort, the pure ease of being with this man. She'd thought they had nothing in common, that their sizzling chemistry was what made it work, but she'd been so, so wrong.

Yes, they were different. She was quick to voice her feelings, while Gage internalized everything. She thought things through, and to some extent, so did he, but he was far more impulsive than her. Like when they'd visited May at the museum the previous weekend—Gage had no qualms about sneaking into an off-limits area to steal a kiss. Or the night they'd gone to grab dinner and he suddenly decided to drive all the way to Portland because he had a craving for lobster, which apparently was only good if you bought it in Maine.

She'd come to appreciate his spontaneity, even look forward to it. Gage had shown her that she could go to work and study but still have fun at the same time. More than that, he made her feel strong and confident, and she loved how bold she'd become because of him.

So bold, in fact, that she didn't even hesitate before sliding her hand over his rock-hard abs to wrap her fingers around his erection. She gave it a teasing tug, eliciting a groan from him.

"You're a sex addict," he grumbled.

"Ha. Like you're complaining."

Still stroking him, she brought her mouth to his for a kiss. His tongue dived through her parted lips and tangled with hers, his hips lifting restlessly as he thrust his cock into her hand.

God, she loved kissing him. Touching him. Watching him come apart.

She let out a disappointed moan when he intercepted her hand, firmly moving it off him. "You never let me have fun," she complained.

"And you always put my pleasure ahead of yours," he said roughly.

"That's because I like pleasing you!"

"Yeah, well, I like pleasing you, too. So be quiet and enjoy." His hand traveled south and stroked her mound, fingers lightly teasing the hood of her clit.

Skyler sighed happily. "Feels so good when you touch me."

"Feels so good to touch you." As he stroked her in a lazy rhythm, his gray eyes burned with what could only be described as adoration.

His middle finger rubbed little circles over her clit, slow and sweet until the pressure between her legs reached an all-time high, causing her to squirm in agitation.

His chuckle fanned over her cheek. "Getting close?"

"Mmm-hmmm."

He moved his hand lower, one long finger sliding inside her as his thumb applied steady pressure on her clit. She cried out when an orgasm swept through her in pulsing ripples, rocking into his hand until the shock waves faded into a warm, delicious afterglow.

Afterward, she nestled against his warm, muscular body, exhaling slowly as that feeling of serenity returned. But even as he pressed a kiss on the top of her head, even as he stroked her hair and held her close, she knew he was still holding back.

Would he ever allow himself to be truly vulnerable around her? Sometimes she wondered. His father and brother had done a number on him, affected his ability to trust anyone but himself, but God, she wished he could trust her enough to fully let her in.

"Gage?"

"Yeah?"

"What are we doing here?"

She felt his chest tense. "What do you mean?"

"You said you don't do relationships, but...well, we've been seeing each other for more than a month." She hesitated, then forced herself to be honest. "This is more than sex to me."

"I know." His voice was husky.

"Are we together? Like, officially together?"

She held her breath as she waited for his answer. As badly as she wanted to hear him say *yes,* she had to wonder if maybe she was forcing things. Fighting for a relationship that was bound to go nowhere. Gage wasn't one of those safe, dependable guys she usually dated, and she couldn't help but feel like she might be in for some major heartbreak.

And yet when he gave a response, she couldn't stop the burst of happiness that went off inside her.

"Yeah," he murmured. "Yeah, we're together."

Her heart did a little somersault. "Good. I like that."

His fingers stroked her hair with infinite tenderness. "Me, too."

Chapter Twelve

As another busy Friday night came to a close, Gage dragged himself up to his office, dead on his feet. He'd broken up five fights tonight, tossed four troublemakers out on their asses, called cabs for half a dozen drunk patrons, and to top it all off, stumbled on a trio of high punks who claimed to have bought the drugs from Sin. Gage and his men still hadn't found the person selling E in the club. Whoever it was had slowed down for a while, but evidently he was back in business.

Exhausted, Gage quickly signed off on his bouncers' shift logs, then wandered down the hall toward Reed's office, wishing like hell he was seeing Skyler tonight. She'd wanted him to come by after work, but he'd insisted that she deserved to go to bed at a reasonable time for a change. They were able to spend time together during the day and on weeknights when the club closed at eleven, but he didn't leave Sin before 3:00 a.m. on the weekends, and he felt bad making her wait up for him.

He knew he'd feel even worse come September — Skyler would be busier then, starting her practicum and seeing patients under the supervision of a licensed psychologist. He'd already vowed not to let his crazy hours affect her ability to work, even if it meant not seeing her as often.

Gage popped his head in the doorway and found Reed at his desk. Still an odd sight, even though he'd had two years to get used to it. Reed was a man of action, so office work seemed completely unsuited for the guy. He tended bar on occasion, but AJ was the one who worked the bar on a nightly basis, while Reed took care of the business end of things.

"I'm heading out," Gage told his partner. "Everything good here?"

Reed glanced up from a mountain of paperwork. "I'm good. Just double-checking these numbers, and then Jerry and I are going to look through some of the old security tapes. We're hoping we might catch our pesky E pusher on tape."

"Let me know if you find anything."

"Will do. 'Night, bro."

"'Night."

Gage left the club through the staff door, rummaging in his pocket as he walked. He wasn't using his e-cig nearly as often anymore, but the craving for nicotine still called to him. He'd been smoking since he was fifteen—worst frickin' mistake of his life—and he was longing for the day when that edgy I-need-a-smoke feeling finally left him for good.

He'd just pulled out the e-cigarette when he heard the footsteps.

Gage's spine went ramrod straight as the shadowy group slunk into the alley. He narrowed his eyes. Eight or so men, and he recognized the ones in front.

Paddy McDougal and Monte O'Brien, two of Mitch's henchman.

"Paddy." Gage spoke in a calm tone. "Monte. What can I do for you guys?"

The wall of thugs formed a menacing semicircle before

him. No visible weapons on any of them, which wasn't surprising. Most of the Irish boys in Southie didn't need guns or knives—their fists were destructive enough.

Drawing an even breath, Gage did a quick assessment of the situation. He was outnumbered eight to one. If they made a move, he could take out at least half of them, maaaaaybe all if he got lucky. But he sincerely doubted they'd allow that. He knew the way these boys fought—hell, he'd sparred with Paddy hundreds of times growing up. O'Donnell's men would fight as a group, one lethal force working together with one goal in mind.

"Mitch has a message for you." Paddy's Irish brogue was soft and deadly. And total bullshit, because Gage knew for a fact that the guy's parents didn't have accents—they'd both been born in Boston, for chrissake.

"Yeah? What's he got to say?" Gage readjusted his stance. He pressed his hands to his sides, letting the cigarette drop into his pocket.

"He wants you to reconsider your thoughts about the tourney."

"I see." He cocked his head. "'Fraid I can't do that. Mitch knows where I stand."

"That's what he figured you'd say." Paddy took an intimidating step forward. Cracked his knuckles, then smiled. "That's where the second part of the message comes in. Mitch is hoping that a couple visits like this might help you change your mind."

Monte, who'd walked to school with Gage every day when they were kids, offered a repentant look. "Nothing personal, man."

Gage exhaled in resignation. "All right. Let's get to it then."

They attacked without warning, Paddy's fist coming at him like a rattlesnake striking its prey. Gage blocked the punch with one hand and clipped Paddy in the jaw with the other. The man's head snapped back, anger clouding his eyes, but Gage was too busy fending off Monte, who'd closed in on him. He got two jabs in, then a well-placed kick in his old friend's crotch. Monte yelped in fury before retaliating, one meaty fist crashing into Gage's left eye.

After that, he was fighting a losing battle. Someone yanked his arms behind his back, locked an iron-strong leg around his knees to keep him in place. Pain streaked through him when he felt another sharp pull on his arm.

Son of a bitch had wrenched his shoulder right out of the socket.

Fucking *hell*, that hurt.

No words echoed in the alley. Just a cacophony of muffled sounds. Thuds, grunts, the sharp smacks of fists against flesh. Gage blocked out the pain, same way he'd blocked it out when he was a kid and his dad was pounding on him. He wasn't sure how long the beating lasted, but eventually he became aware of other noises. Footsteps. Shouts. Suddenly he was sagging forward, falling to his knees as his head swam and his pulse shrieked in his ears.

"Get the *fuck* out of here!" Reed's voice. Coming from far, far away.

Gage blinked, trying to pinpoint where Reed was, but one eye was swollen shut and the other made out nothing but blurry shapes. He tasted copper in his mouth, felt moisture dripping down his chin, but he was too dazed to spit the blood out or wipe it away.

"Gage. *Gage*. You okay, man?" Reed again, concern ringing from his voice.

He cranked open his good eye, relief flooding his body when his friend's face came into focus. "F-fine," he croaked out. "I'm fine."

"…ambulance," he heard someone say. It sounded like

Jerry.

"No." Gage wheezed, struggling to catch his breath. "No hospitals." He tried to get up, but his ribs ached like a motherfucker, shooting jolts of pain through his chest. A few were most likely broken. And yup, his shoulder was definitely dislocated, dangling uselessly as he managed to get on his feet.

"Gage. You're fucked up," Reed said firmly. "You need to get looked at."

"I'm good," he mumbled as he battled a rush of dizziness. "Just pop my shoulder back in, will ya?"

Disbelief echoed in his friend's voice. "Sweet Jesus. You're nuts."

He stumbled toward the wall. "I'll do it myself then."

"Oh, for chrissake." He caught a flash of movement in the corner of his eye. "Jerry, get over here."

"Shouldn't he be lying down for this?" their security guy demanded, equally dumbfounded.

"Yeah, but do *you* want to try to get this stubborn idiot to follow orders?"

Gage felt himself being moved, and then his arm was being lifted and hot agony rippled through him. Reed's strong grip slowly pulled on his biceps, shifting his arm away from his torso. He bit the inside of his cheek so violently he tasted more blood in his mouth.

"You good, bro?"

"Just…do…it," he said through clenched teeth.

The tension was unbearable. His shoulder burned, ached, pulsed with agony, and then a sickening crack sliced the air, and pain mingled with relief as the joint popped back into place.

As his vision blurred again, he leaned into Reed with a groan. "No…hospitals." He felt himself losing consciousness. Fought it. Kept talking. "Just…take me home."

"God, I really hate you sometimes," Reed mumbled.

The black dots in front of his face got worse, an undulating sea of darkness beckoning at him. "One more thing."

"Demanding bastard tonight, aren't ya? What is it?"

They were in motion now, Gage's bulk supported by Jerry and Reed as they carried him out of the alley. He had the vague impression of the sidewalk beneath his feet, but couldn't seem to make his eyes focus.

"Skyler…" He swallowed, wincing from the taste of blood coating his throat. "Don't call her…don't…she can't know… promise."

"Goddamn it, Gage—"

"*Promise.*"

There was a pause, then Reed's unhappy voice. "I promise."

Gage nodded gratefully.

And passed the fuck out.

• • •

If it were anyone else calling, Skyler probably would have slept through the ringing of her phone, but she'd programmed a personal ringtone for Gage, and somehow her subconscious knew it. Her eyes snapped open and sought out the bedside clock. When she realized it was four in the morning, instant concern swept through her. She knew Gage wouldn't call so late if it weren't important.

She picked up immediately—and was startled when a voice that didn't belong to Gage filled her ear.

"Skyler? It's Reed."

Her stomach clenched. Oh God. Something must be seriously wrong if Gage's best friend was on the line.

"What happened?" she blurted out. "Is he okay?" The slight hesitation on the other end sent her heart rate into overtime. "*Reed.* Tell me what happened."

"O'Donnell's crew roughed him up."

She swallowed a cold rush of fear. "How bad?"

"Bad. And the muleheaded mofo refused to go to the hospital, so I took him home. Can you—"

"I'm on my way."

She hung up without another word and proceeded to dress in a panicky whirlwind, throwing on the first items of clothing she found. Then she flew down the stairs toward Lacey's room, only to halt in her tracks when she remembered that her friend was at the hospital. Damn it. Lacey was a doctor—Skyler would have felt a million times better if her friend had been able to check on Gage with her.

How badly was he hurt? Why hadn't he called her himself? Terrified thoughts buzzed through her mind as she slid into her car. Since it was so late, there was zero traffic on the road, but she forced herself not to drive double the speed limit. She couldn't afford to get pulled over by a cop right now.

Panic and worry sizzled in her veins the entire way to Gage's house. When she got there, all the lights were on, and Reed met her at the front door, his blue eyes grim.

"He's in the living room."

She was already pushing past him. She didn't take off her shoes, just careened into the living room. Her heart plummeted to the pit of her stomach when she saw Gage.

He was on the couch, flat on his back with his eyes closed. Well, with one eye closed—the other was swollen shut, black and purple and twice its normal size. Her breathing grew shallow as she examined the rest of him. A cut on his eyebrow, held together by a row of narrow butterfly stitches. More bluish bruises on his bare chest, white tape wrapped tightly around his torso. His hands were at his sides, and from where she stood, she noticed his knuckles were red and caked with blood.

Reed's voice drifted in from the doorway. "We cleaned

him up, taped up his ribs, and shoved some aspirin down his throat."

Skyler sat next to Gage and gently touched the cheek that wasn't bruised. He didn't stir, massive chest rising and falling with each steady inhale and exhale.

"He was probably right about the hospital," Reed added, albeit grudgingly. "The doctors wouldn't have done much more than Jerry and I did. None of the cuts are deep enough for stitches, and there's nothing they can do for his ribs."

Skyler swallowed, then shifted her gaze to Reed. Another man stood next to him. Their employee Jerry, she assumed. "You guys can go," she said softly. "I'll stay here with him."

Reed's forehead creased. "You sure?"

She nodded. "Go. We both know he wouldn't like having all of us fussing over him. It'll just make him grumpy."

Reed's lips twitched in a reluctant smile. "You're right about that." He walked over and dropped a quick kiss on her forehead. "Good luck with our patient. Though I have a feeling he'll be grumpy regardless."

Yeah, so did she, but there was no way in hell she was going anywhere.

She moved her attention back to Gage, effectively dismissing the other men. She heard their footsteps in the hall, the creak of the front door closing, but her focus remained on Gage. She squeezed his hand, then dipped her head and pressed her lips to his in a tender kiss. He still didn't stir, and she didn't try to rouse him. He needed to rest right now.

But there was no rest for Skyler. She stretched out beside him, keeping an inch of space between them as she settled on her side and watched him breathe. Tears stung her eyes when she started cataloging all his cuts and bruises again.

Gage had been so certain Mitch O'Donnell had accepted that their arrangement was over, but obviously he'd been wrong. So fucking wrong. O'Donnell had gone out and punished him for not toeing the line, and Skyler fought the urge to track that bastard down and strangle the life out of him.

As she mentally plotted O'Donnell's demise, an uneasy thought occurred to her. Clay could help.

No, Clay *would* help, if she only asked him.

But did she really want to reach out to the man who'd brought chaos into her family and uprooted her entire life?

You wouldn't do it for Gage?

She pressed her lips together, trying to keep a sob at bay. God, that wasn't even a question. Of course she'd go to Clay if it meant helping Gage. She'd do *anything* to stop O'Donnell from hurting the man she loved.

Skyler froze.

The man she *loved*?

Her heart beat faster as she stared at Gage's face, still unbelievably gorgeous despite being all bruised up. But even from the start, it had been about more than his looks. It was his intensity, his strength, his dominance. It was the thrilling sex and the sweet kisses. The way he appealed to her nurturing side and fueled her confidence and challenged her to unleash her wild side. Her previous boyfriends hadn't done that. They'd been content with the status quo, the same old date nights followed by the same predictable sex.

Gage, on the other hand, was not at all predictable.

She loved him, damn it. She loved his gruff voice and his dirty words, the roughness of his touch, his rare smiles and even rarer laughter. Maybe he wasn't the most open person, but she was so much closer to unlocking him, she could *feel* it. And had no doubt that when he finally let her in, she'd love him even more.

Somehow during her train of thought, she must have fallen asleep, because when she opened her eyes, sunlight was streaming in through the curtainless windows. It was morning.

And Gage was groaning, she realized.

The hoarse sound shot her into a sitting position. She quickly wiped the sleep from her eyes just as his opened. He looked disoriented for a moment.

"Sky?" he rasped.

"I'm here." She touched his cheek in a soothing motion, startled to see him flinch. But not from pain. No, his eyes were swimming with…unhappiness?

"I told him not to call you," Gage mumbled.

She wrinkled her brow. "You told Reed not to call me?"

Another groan. "Gonna…kill him."

"Don't you dare." She pinned him with a fierce glare. "If he hadn't called, I would've kicked his ass. This is exactly where I need to be, right here by your side."

His third groan sounded like it was mingled with the word "no," but she decided she'd misheard him.

Skyler hopped off the couch and smoothed out her tangled hair. "I'll get you some water."

"No."

Now she heard it loud and clear. She frowned when he attempted to sit up. "Don't move," she said firmly. "You're just going to jostle your ribs and make them hurt worse."

The insufferable man ignored the command, sliding up until his back rested against the arm of the couch. "Sky…" The unhappy look returned, clouding his gray eyes.

"Don't argue with me," she grumbled. "I'm getting you some water, and then making you something to eat." She crossed her arms. "I know you don't like accepting help, but I'm here to take care of you."

"No."

The word ripped out of his throat once more, bringing a pang of uneasiness. "Why not?"

He rubbed his fist over his good eye before peering helplessly at her. "Damn it, Skyler. You can't be here."

Disbelief spiraled through her. "Where the hell else would I be?"

He went quiet for so long she wondered if he'd say anything at all. But then he did, and her entire world rocked on its axis.

"I want you to go."

"Why, damn it?"

"Because…" He was breathing hard. "I can't do this anymore."

"You don't know what you're saying. It's just the painkillers talking."

"I didn't take any painkillers. I know exactly what I'm saying, baby."

Tears pricked her eyes. She knew she shouldn't ask, but evidently she was a glutton for self-punishment, because the question burst out anyway. "What *are* you saying?"

"I'm saying it's over."

Chapter Thirteen

Gage felt like a dozen fists had pummeled his chest repeatedly—and it had nothing to do with the fact that eight men had literally done that to him last night.

It was the devastation in Skyler's beautiful blue eyes that evoked the beat-to-shit feeling. He'd known he'd end up hurting her, but knowing and seeing it happen were two very different things. Two very different levels of pure agony and total self-loathing.

But he couldn't turn away from the course he'd set. He wasn't good enough for her, he'd known it from the start, and it couldn't have been clearer now, not if it was written in neon and flashing in Times Square. He was black and blue, courtesy of some very dangerous men, and he knew damn well that O'Donnell's crew wasn't going to leave him alone.

Christ, he'd been a naive fool. Thinking that Mitch would happily let their arrangement come to an end. Ha. The bastard would keep coming after him until he got what he wanted from Gage. If it struck his sick fancy, he'd even use Skyler to get it, and there was no way in hell Gage would let O'Donnell hurt her.

"Are you saying this because of Mitch? Are you ending it to protect me?" As usual, the damned woman read his mind.

"Partly," he admitted.

"Well, that's *bullshit*." It was rare to hear her swear, and with such vehemence, too. "You don't need to play the hero, and if you're really worried he'll come after you—or me—we can get the cops involved. Get a restraining order. There are lots of things we can do that don't involve breaking up!"

"Skyler—"

Her eyes blazed with determination as she cut him off. "I can call my stepfather. Clay works for the—"

"This isn't just about Mitch," Gage interrupted. "I'm trying to protect you from *me*."

She faltered, blinking in confusion.

"I'm not good enough for you." His throat closed up. He'd never felt this helpless in his life. "Don't you get it? I'm a punk from Southie who grew up to be an emotionally detached bastard. You deserve better."

Skyler's jaw tightened. "There you go again, telling me what I need. I can make my own decisions, Gage—and I choose to be with you."

"I won't let you." He set his own jaw, and ignored the resulting ache that pulsed through his face.

One eye was still out of commission, but the other worked just fine, and he clearly saw the cloud of despair darkening Skyler's eyes. Lord, she was beautiful. Beautiful and vulnerable and sweet and strong. Stronger than he'd thought, sure, but she was owed better than a man who was tangled up with thugs, a man who couldn't truly open up to her. Lowering his guard during sex was one thing, but the intimacy she needed—no, the intimacy she *deserved*? He wasn't sure he'd ever be able to give it to her.

That sappy phrase suddenly floated into his mind, the one

about loving someone enough to let them go. Well, he loved Skyler. He loved her strength, her intelligence, her endless compassion, and most of all, her light.

The light he'd eventually extinguish.

"I can't be the kind of man you need." His throat burned so badly he could barely get a word out. "You need someone who's open and talks about important stuff, someone who smiles and laughs. That's not me. I shut down years ago."

"You've been opening up. I've seen it. I've *felt* it." Desperation clung to her voice.

"It's not enough. It'll never be enough." Gage staggered off the couch, light-headed and sick to his stomach. When Skyler took a step forward, he held up his hand to stop her. "No, I'm fine."

Her eyes flashed again. "God. You can't ever accept help, can you? Would it *kill* you to let someone help you?"

Frustration slammed into him like a sledgehammer. It was the same accusation he'd heard a hundred times before. "See?" he said miserably. "It's happening already. If we keep this up, you'll end up resenting me. I *can't* be the man you want me to be."

"I want you to be you," she burst out. "I don't want you to change—I just want you to trust me enough to show me the real you. The good parts, the bad parts, just *you*." She stopped abruptly, realization dawning in her eyes. "But you don't trust anyone, do you? You can't trust anyone, not completely."

Swallowing, Gage slowly shook his head.

"Then you're right." A defeated breath shuddered out of her mouth, her shoulders sagging as if they were carrying the weight of the world. "We don't stand a chance."

A fiery rush of pain slid through him, but he couldn't argue with her. They hadn't stood a chance from the beginning.

Goddamn it. He should've followed his own frickin' ground rules. Keep things light, keep it all about sex. Maybe if he'd stuck to his guns, he wouldn't feel like someone had ripped his chest open and was prodding at his heart with a pair of rusty pliers.

"I'm sorry," he whispered.

"Yeah. So am I." Skyler looked so sad he almost charged forward and pulled her into his arms, but he forced himself to stay motionless.

After a long, agonizing moment, she came up and brushed a featherlight kiss on his lips. "Good-bye, Gage."

His throat was too tight to answer, so he settled for a jerky nod.

He'd expected the pain, the accusation, the anger. But it was the disappointment in her eyes that ripped him to shreds.

That disappointment was the last thing he saw before she walked out of the room, and out of his life.

. . .

Stupid, stupid, stupid.

The chiding internal voice followed Skyler all the way out to her car. Somehow, her legs carried her there without buckling. Somehow, she got in the driver's seat without collapsing.

God, she should have seen it sooner, but she'd convinced herself that Gage was letting her in. That slowly but surely she'd succeed in earning his trust.

But she hadn't realized that trust was unattainable. She'd been chasing a pot of gold at the end of the rainbow. Trusting someone—*really* trusting them—meant letting yourself be truly vulnerable, and Gage had banished those emotions at a young age.

She'd been a fool to think something as silly as love would change that.

Her fingers shook as she turned the key in the ignition.

She drove away from his town house with tears in her eyes, wondering where the hell she would even go. She didn't want to return to her empty house, which made her realize just how much she'd enjoyed having Gage in her life, how much she'd loved having someone to spend time with, to talk to. She had two roommates, but she might as well have been living alone.

Hospital or museum. Those were her options. Lacey and May would let her cry on their shoulders and listen to her vent, something she desperately needed to do at the moment.

Ten minutes later, she found herself pulling into a parking spot that didn't belong to either Boston General or the city's modern art museum.

Skyler blinked. She'd unconsciously driven to her stepfather's house in Beacon Hill.

With tears marring her vision, she studied the luxury town house, with its stately brick facade and colonial-style architecture. She and her mother had moved into the house after the divorce, and Skyler couldn't have gotten out of there faster. After high school graduation, she'd moved into her college dorm, never to spend another night in Clay's house. Since her mother's death, she hadn't even been back for a visit.

But she got out of the car now and headed for the front door to ring the bell. She swiped her sleeve over her wet eyes as she waited on the stoop. God, what was she doing here? There was still time to go, if she hurried back to her car before—

The door swung open, revealing her stepfather's shocked face.

"Sky?" His eyes widened when he noticed the tears staining her cheeks. "Are you okay? Come inside, sweetheart. Come in."

He ushered her into the front hall, closed the door, and pulled her into his bulky arms before she could voice a protest.

Skyler stiffened for a beat before sagging into the embrace. They hadn't hugged in years, and the hugs they *had* shared always felt forced and awkward. No matter how hard her mother had begged her to give Clay a chance, Skyler had never been able to warm up to him.

Her father had been gentle and compassionate, but Clay was the complete opposite. Commanding and hardened after years of heading up the organized crime unit in the FBI's Boston field office. He'd swept into her mother's life like a movie hero, an exciting man with a dangerous career, and Skyler's mother had welcomed it. She'd fallen head over heels for him, leaving Skyler's father in the dust.

"What's wrong, sweetheart?" Clay released her and cupped her cheeks.

"Nothing." She gulped. "I mean, not nothing. But you don't have to worry. I'm okay."

His eyes narrowed. "Why are you crying?"

"I…a friend of mine was…he got hurt last night…and…" She searched Clay's familiar face, rugged planes, thick dark eyebrows, strong mouth. "I need a favor."

"Anything."

The response was so swift it elicited a rush of guilt. The man had tried hard to form a connection with her and she'd fought him every step of the way, and yet when she came to him for help, he gave it so freely she felt like crying again.

"Come on, let's go to the kitchen. Do you want some coffee? I just brewed a pot."

A minute later, she settled on a stool at the eat-in breakfast counter, where a steaming mug already sat. Her heart cracked in two when she noticed it was the mug she'd given Clay for his birthday years ago. Her mom had wanted her to pick one with a cheesy phrase on it—*I love my stepdaddy* had actually been available at the store—but Skyler had ignored the pleas and chosen one with a black-and-white picture of Boston's harbor instead. Simple, boring.

Impersonal.

The fact that he was drinking from it, all these years later, made her feel like the most dreadful person on the planet.

"Tell me what happened to your friend," Clay said in his no-nonsense voice. He handed her a cup of coffee, then sat down across from her.

Skyler took a breath. She wasn't sure if what she was asking was even possible, but she had to try. For Gage. They might have ended it, but that didn't mean she wanted to see him get hurt again. He deserved to be free of O'Donnell, and if she could help him achieve that, she'd damn well do it.

"Have you ever heard of a man named Mitch O'Donnell? Supposedly he's a local businessman, but he's involved in the drug business and probably a bunch of other illegal stuff."

Clay's expression turned deadly. "I know all about O'Donnell." He cursed. "How the hell did you get mixed up with him, Sky? The man has ties to the Irish mafia—my unit has been keeping an eye on him for years."

She wasn't at all surprised to hear it. "I thought you'd know him."

"Tell me what happened."

After a moment of hesitation, she met her stepfather's eyes and told him everything. About Gage's brother, about the deal he'd struck, about the beating. When she finished, Clay looked unhappy, and more than a little worried.

"This friend of yours…is he your boyfriend?"

She shook her head, ignoring the tight vise of pain squeezing her heart. "He's just a friend. And I want to help him. I want O'Donnell to leave him alone. Can you help? Maybe put some pressure on him, or threaten to arrest him if he goes after Gage again?"

Clay ran a hand through his graying hair, his expression conveying visible reluctance.

"Please," she begged. "I…" She took a breath. "I know I haven't been the best stepdaughter on the planet, but I promise I'll make more of an effort. It's just…"

His eyes went sad. "You blame me for your parents splitting up."

She managed a shaky nod. "I know it's not entirely your fault, and I know my dad's heart attack didn't have to do with the divorce, but…I'm trying, Clay. I really am trying to see past what you and my mom did."

"I know. That's why I've never pushed you. You're a good person, Sky, and you've got such a big heart." His voice cracked. "I know eventually you'll open that heart to me, and I'm willing to wait as long as it takes. I loved your mother, I hope you believe that, but I love you too. I don't have any other kids. You're my daughter, whether you like me or not." He offered a faint grin. "I'm afraid you're stuck with me, kid."

His words triggered another spurt of tears. God. It suddenly occurred to her that he was right. She'd lost both of her parents, didn't have any other family. *Clay* was all she had.

"I'll try harder," she vowed. "And not because I need your help. Even if you said no right now, I'd still try." Squaring her jaw, she gestured to the carton of eggs sitting on the other counter. "In fact, why don't we start with breakfast?"

"I like the sound of that." Smiling, Clay rose from the stool. "Do you still like your eggs scrambled?"

She smiled. "Yep."

As he headed for the counter, his demeanor turned serious again. "As for our little O'Donnell problem, you don't have to worry, Sky. I'll take care of it."

Relief spiraled through her. "Thank you."

And then she stood up and went to help her stepfather prepare breakfast.

Chapter Fourteen

Two weeks later

"Oh Jesus, don't tell me you're going to fight in that tourney!" Reed's outraged voice blared from the doorway, right as Gage's fist slammed into the center of the punching bag hanging in the corner of his office.

He pulled his arm back and glanced over, forehead wrinkling in bewilderment. "Of course not."

Reed strode inside. "Yeah? Because it sure as hell looks like you're training for something. You've been beating the crap out of that bag every evening before we open."

Gage grabbed the towel on the desk chair and mopped up the sweat rolling down his bare chest. "I'm not training. I'm just letting off steam."

Ha. Letting off steam. That was a nice way to phrase it. Truth was, he was spiraling. Free-falling without a parachute and trying to grab on to anything to ground him.

He missed Skyler so much it hurt. He figured pounding a bag of sand was better than walking around like a dead man.

He hadn't realized how big of a part she'd come to play in his life until she was gone. The phone calls. The movie marathons. Teaching her to cook. Talking. Fucking.

Lord, he felt empty without her, but he was forcing himself not to second-guess his decision to end it. Although Mitch and his men hadn't come after him again, Gage knew it was only a matter of time. Which was just another reason to stay in shape—the next time they made a move, he'd be ready for it.

Except he wouldn't wait for them to come to *him* this time. He'd decided that this morning, when he'd yet again woken up alone in a bed that still smelled like Skyler because he refused to change the sheets. He wanted to hold on to her sweet fragrance for as long as he could, to cling to the memory of how much he'd loved holding her, kissing her, moving inside her.

"Then you still haven't heard from Mitch?" Reed asked.

Gage tossed the towel aside. He ignored the lingering ache in his rib cage as he pulled on a T-shirt. "Nope. But he's about to hear from me."

AJ drifted into the office at that moment, his expression hardening as he caught Gage's remark. "Wait, what? Did you just say you're going after O'Donnell?"

"I want to set up a meeting." He shrugged. "Make it clear that he isn't in control of my life. I'm not his puppet, and I won't fight on command."

"You really think he'll just happily agree to back off?" Reed gestured to Gage's face. "Bro, you're still sporting the bruises from your last meeting with his crew."

"They can rough me up as much as they want. Mitch needs to know I won't play ball, no matter how much he pushes." Setting his shoulders, Gage went over to the desk and searched for his phone.

"If you're serious about meeting with him, then we're

coming with you," AJ said firmly.

His friend's don't-even-think-of-arguing tone surprised him. AJ had been a professional fighter, just like Gage and Reed, but the man lacked the violent streak that ran freely through his two friends. With his dark blond hair and twinkling green eyes, AJ was the easygoing, boy-next-door type. Too damn nice for his own good, which was why Gage had been surprised to run into him on the fighting circuit—until he'd seen him in the cage and realized just how deadly AJ Walsh could be. Still, although AJ craved the adrenaline high he got in the cage, once he left it he reverted back to Mr. Nice Guy.

"Damn right we are," Reed agreed. "We're not letting you anywhere near that psycho without backup."

"I'm not arguing with you." Gage gave his friends a wry grin. "I was already planning on recruiting you to come along." He found his phone under a stack of time sheets, the grin fading as he pulled up Mitch's number.

A few seconds later, O'Donnell answered with an angry, "What the fuck do you want, Holt?"

Gage was taken aback by the curt tone. "Mitch. I figured it was time the two of us had a little chat."

A derisive snort echoed in his ear. "Don't worry, I got the message loud and clear."

His confusion intensified. "Message?"

"Yeah, you know, when you sicced your own private Fed on me? Special Agent Rivers made it clear what would happen if I didn't back off. And you know me, I'm all about self-preservation. I can't have the organized crime unit putting a spotlight on me, so slap yourself on the back, asshole. Looks like we're out of each other's lives for good."

Although he had no clue what O'Donnell was blabbing about, Gage couldn't help but voice a stern caveat. "That includes Denny. You leave him alone, too."

"The two of you could rot in hell for all I care. Have a

good life, Holt."

Click.

He stared at the phone, his brain working overtime to make sense of the conversation, until finally it dawned on him. Special Agent Rivers. As in *Clay* Rivers. The same name Gage had glimpsed on Skyler's phone numerous times before, when she was ignoring another one of her stepfather's texts.

"Son of a bitch," he breathed.

"What is it?" Reed appeared in front of him, wariness etched on his chiseled face.

"Skyler." He drew in a breath. "She…"

She'd gone to bat for him. He remembered her trying to tell him where her stepfather worked, but he'd cut her off, and now it was painfully apparent. Clay Rivers was a federal agent.

And Skyler had gotten him to help Gage.

The startling truth achieved an impossible feat inside him—his heart was unbelievably full and desolately empty at the same damn time.

"Her stepfather's in the FBI," Gage told his friends, hearing the note of awe in his voice. "Somehow he convinced O'Donnell to back off. Probably threatened him with something."

Because of Skyler.

Skyler.

His brain refused to let go of that tidbit. The sheer gravity of what she'd done for him wasn't lost, either. She'd reached out to a man she was estranged from just to help Gage.

You can't ever accept help, can you? Would it kill *you to let someone help you?*

Her words came back to him now, slamming into his head with the force of a freight train. Even after Gage had broken up with her, she'd put her own pain and issues aside to ask her stepfather for help.

"I need to see her," he mumbled. "I need to get her back."

A soft chuckle left Reed's lips. "No kidding."

Christ. He was such an idiot. Skyler was the best thing that had ever happened to him. She'd been open with him from the start, unafraid to show him every part of herself, even the parts she thought were bad. She'd shared everything with him. She never hid *anything*.

And now it was time for him to stop hiding, too.

. . .

Skyler's pen flew over her notepad as she scribbled down drink orders for a table of recently graduated high schoolers celebrating the start of college. School would be starting up again in a couple weeks, but not for her. She'd be working in the field now, treating actual patients at the North End women's center where the university had placed her. Sure, she'd be working under the supervision of another therapist, but the thought of talking to real people and helping them with their problems still thrilled her.

But not as much as the sight of Gage walking into the restaurant. As always, she'd sensed his presence, swiveling her head in time for their gazes to collide from across the room.

It was unbelievably unfair that he could still evoke such a visceral response in her. Make her heart pound and her palms tingle from his mere proximity.

They hadn't seen or spoken to each other in two weeks, and she hadn't realized just how badly she'd missed him until this very moment. She wanted to drop her order pad and sprint over to him, throw her arms around his neck, and kiss the living daylights out of him.

But she couldn't. Nope, because he'd broken up with her. Jerk.

Skyler forced herself to concentrate on her customers, but

the second she'd finished taking their order, she hurried over to the drink station and latched her hand on Megan's arm.

"Do you mind bringing these drinks over to table five?" she asked the other waitress, thrusting out the order pad. "I need to take a five-minute break."

"No prob, hon." Megan's gaze drifted toward the hostess stand, a smile forming on her lips. "Take ten, if you need it."

"Thanks. I owe you one." A moment later, she hurriedly crossed the busy room toward Gage. "What are you doing here?" she asked when she reached him.

His gray eyes held a serious gleam. "I needed to talk to you."

She managed a nod. "All right. Let's go somewhere private."

"No. I don't care who hears this."

Skyler raised a brow. Okay, that was weird. A word-stingy, private man like Gage wanting to talk in earshot of everyone? And there were a lot of ears in their vicinity. Like the ones belonging to Rita, the restaurant's nosy hostess. Or the six frat boys in the booth directly to their left, who were making no effort to hide their curious stares.

"I..." Gage cleared his throat. "I wanted to thank you. I know what you did, asking your stepfather to deal with O'Donnell, and...well, thank you."

"You're welcome." When he fell silent, she lifted her eyebrows again. "Is that all you wanted?"

He shook his head. "I also wanted to say...uh..." Something flashed in his eyes. Determination. Maybe fortitude. Whatever it was, it seemed to push him to keep going. "Sky...I have issues."

An unwitting grin sprang to her lips. "No kidding."

He sighed. "Don't be a brat. I'm being serious."

"Sorry. Go on." But her lips continued to twitch.

"Look, my childhood sucked, okay? I'm not whining about it—it is what it is. But I can't deny that it screwed with my head." His voice contained that gruff note she loved so much. "I've taken care of myself for so long I don't know how to ask for help. I've never counted on anyone before. I've never *needed* anyone before." His throat bobbed as he swallowed. "It's hard for me to lean on anyone, because nobody has ever been there for me to lean on. And the people who *were* there? I couldn't trust them."

When he stopped and bit his lip, it was so damn adorable she almost dived into his arms, but she forced herself to wait for him to finish.

"But I trust *you*," he said huskily. "I trust you, baby. And I need you."

Her heart soared. "You do?"

He nodded, then stepped closer and stroked her cheek with his callused thumb. His gaze was earnest as it fixed on hers. "I love you, Skyler. I love every goddamn thing about you, and I promise you, if you give me another chance, I'll show you what I was too afraid to show you before. *Me*."

Aw, hell. Her eyes were leaking. She was actually going to cry in the middle of her place of business.

"Dude," a male voice cracked, "this is some real *Jerry Maguire* shit over here."

Gage jabbed a thumb in the direction of the frat booth. "Shut it. I'm trying to win back my girl."

His girl. God, Skyler didn't think she'd ever heard more beautiful words.

"Is it working?" Gage asked, turning back to her.

His sheepish expression, combined with the love shining in his eyes, melted away all the hurt and anger and longing she'd been plagued with these past two weeks.

Grinning, she grasped his chin between her hands and said, "You had me at hello."

A round of groans erupted from the booth, along with veral loud remarks all featuring the word "cheesy," but

Skyler was too focused on Gage to care.

The smile that filled his face stole the breath right out of her lungs, and then he was kissing her, those incredible lips brushing over hers before disappearing much too soon.

When she tried to pull him close again, he chuckled and murmured a reminder. "You're at work."

Right. She'd totally forgotten. "I get off in an hour. Will you wait for me until I'm done?"

The smile never left his face. "Damn straight."

When he took a step in the direction of the bar, she grabbed the front of his T-shirt and shot him a stern look. "Two more things."

Gage waited expectantly.

"One...I love you, too."

His breath hitched, and the joy that flooded his gaze was the most wondrous thing she'd ever seen.

"And two..." She moved close again, bringing her lips to his ear. "If you think you're off the hook for breaking up with me, think again, big guy. I plan on punishing you the second we get home."

Those gray eyes darkened with heat. He shifted his head, his five o'clock shadow scraping her cheek as his mouth slid over hers in another brief kiss. "Yeah?" he said, sounding intrigued. "What kind of punishment can I expect?"

"Sex," she whispered into his ear. "Lots and lots of sex."

A seductive chuckle slid out of his mouth. "Bring it on, bad girl. Bring it on."

About the Author

A RITA-award-nominated, bestselling author, Elle Kennedy grew up in the suburbs of Toronto, Ontario, and holds a BA in English from York University. From an early age, she knew she wanted to be a writer, and actively began pursuing that dream when she was a teenager. She loves strong heroines and sexy alpha heroes, and just enough heat and danger to keep things interesting!

Elle loves to hear from her readers. Visit her website www.ellekennedy.com or sign up for her newsletter to receive updates about upcoming books and exclusive excerpts. You can also find her on Facebook or follow her on Twitter (@ ElleKennedy).

If you love sexy romance, one-click these steamy Brazen releases...

Owned by Fate
a *Serve* novel by Tessa Bailey

Journalist Caroline Preston arrives at Serve, the city's hottest BDSM club, with one goal—to hate it. But then she sees him. Ripped. Rough. Eyes that could incinerate a girl's panties. As the owner of the club, Jonah Briggs sole purpose is to ensure that his clientele get everything they need, but when he sees Caroline, his only thought is what he wants—to give the sexy little reporter the most exquisite pleasure she's ever experienced...if she'll let him.

Down on Her Knees
a *Dare Me* novel by Christine Bell

Detective Rafe Davenport makes Courtney DeLollis uneasy. She knows all too well what happens when a man has too much control, but a deeper, darker part of her is fascinated by his need to dominate in the bedroom. So when Rafe dares her to try four scenes, each designed to tease and torment, Courtney reluctantly agrees. But once he has her on her knees, Rafe realizes that she might be the one woman capable of bringing him to his...

Two Week Seduction
a novel by Kathy Lyons

Former bad boy turned Tech Sergeant John O'Donnell has exactly two weeks to sort out his mother's finances before he heads back overseas—two weeks that he's determined to spend as far from his best friend's little sister as possible. Alea Heling has been craving more from John since their wild days together in high school, and this time, she's not taking no for an answer... even if John won't let it become more. Even if more is what they both need.

Protecting What's His
a *Line of Duty* novel by Tessa Bailey

Sassy bartender Ginger Peet just committed the perfect crime. Life-sized Dolly Parton statue in tow, Ginger and her sister flee Nashville. But their new neighbor, straight-laced Chicago homicide cop Derek Tyler, knows something's up—something *big*—and he won't rest until Ginger's safe...and in his bed for good.

Printed in Great Britain
by Amazon